Castor heard the door click shut and, still lying chained to the table, he felt the poison starting to work its way through him.

His mouth started to foam, like something rabid.

His whole body shuddered, hot and then cold.

His legs stiffened, splaying out to the sides.

His nails became harder and sharper and thicker, and they pushed out from his paws, so long they began to curl under.

His back arched, the fur standing on end as the feathers started to poke through and unfurl. It felt like sharp, tiny claws were scratching, trying to push out of his shoulders. And it felt like his whole spine was snapping in half.

UNNATURALS
THE BATTLE BEGINS

DEVON HUGHES

Illustrated by
Owen Richardson

KATHERINE TEGEN BOOKS
An Imprint of HarperCollins Publishers

Katherine Tegen Books is an imprint of HarperCollins Publishers.

Unnaturals: The Battle Begins
Text copyright © 2015 by HarperCollins Publishers
Jacket and interior artwork © 2014 by Owen Richardson
For information address HarperCollins Children's Books,
a division of HarperCollins Publishers, 195 Broadway,
New York, NY 10007.
www.harpercollinschildrens.com

Library of Congress Cataloging-in-Publication Data
Hughes, Devon.
The battle begins / Devon Hughes. — First edition.
    pages cm
    Summary: "When Castor the street dog is captured, he learns there is
a nefarious underground fighting ring in Lion's Head where animals
are injected with DNA-changing serums, transformed into dangerous
hybrids, and forced to battle one another to survive"— Provided by
publisher.
    ISBN 978-0-06-225755-0
    [1. Dogs—Fiction. 2. Genetic engineering—Fiction. 3. Dogfighting—
Fiction. 4. Science fiction.] I. Title.
PZ7.1.H82Bat 2015   2014041257
[Fic]—dc23   CIP
                                                              AC

17 18 19 20 21 OPM 10 9 8 7 6 5 4 3 2 1
❖
First paperback edition, 2017

This book is dedicated to my editors,
Melissa Miller and Claudia Gabel,
who've earned it
a thousand times over.
—DH

PROLOGUE

This is where it starts—where it always starts: you peer out over your long nose and see green.

It brushes against your outer coat and tickles the smooth skin of your belly. It blankets the ground beneath your paws. In place of the endless stone boxes the men built, giant green trunks rise up around you. You sit on your hindquarters but still can't quite tilt your head back far enough to see their leafy tops.

This isn't your home. There's no way you could've been here before. But somehow, it feels familiar. And there is something else you recognize. . . .

Meat.

Your whole body seems to shout the word at once. Fur bristles along your spine. Your muzzle twitches and saliva drips from your jowls. You feel the smooth sharpness of your tearing teeth. It has been so long.

Where is the meat?

Your ears stand upright, the fine hairs taking in everything. You hear the crisp snap of a small branch, then the whisper of fur brushing against leaves. You think you can even hear the trill of a heartbeat.

More than anything, though, you can smell the creature, hidden in the shadows, between the darker shades of green. It smells like fear and food, like everything you love about the chase. It smells like life.

Out of the corner of your vision, you sense motion. You spring forward from your back legs, and the animal bolts, a tawny blur.

It's not like the rodents you're used to. This is bigger. It bounds instead of skitters, leaps instead of burrows. It's all speed and grace, and you love the energy it takes to chase after it.

Your pack is with you suddenly—brothers and sisters and second cousins, alphas and omegas. As you tear through the forest, head nodding and eyes watering, they trail in lines behind you, and you know without looking that your tail is streaming out like a flag. With the blood pumping inside your ears, each second sounds like a bark.

The creature is faster than you are, but it's losing steam. You're panting but not tired. You run and run and run, watching the spindly legs flick through the underbrush ahead of you.

You were made for this.

There's a flick of white, a flash of a hoof. You drive harder, your nails churning up cool dirt. The pack fans out and starts to close in, herding your prey closer and closer.

It's slowing. You're gaining. It stumbles, and you dive.

You open your jaws.

You sink in your teeth.

You savor.

ALPHAS AND OMEGAS

ALPHAS
AND
OMEGAS

"In Unnatural World, the Invincible Reigns On!"

"Shocking End to Mega Monster Mash-up!"

"Next Season's Mutants:
Vote Now for Your Dream DNA Mix!"

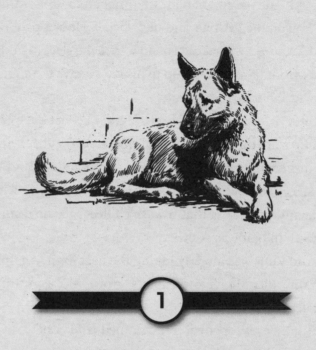

1

A TERRIBLE, HIGH-PITCHED YELP SLICED THROUGH THE dream, and Castor scrambled onto four legs, disoriented.

It was the hottest part of the day—which, in Lion's Head, meant hot—and most of the dogs in Castor's pack were still stretched in lazy heaps, trying to grab a bit of shade and some sleep.

Not Alpha, though. Alpha was wide-awake, facing the far side of the pack, where the scrawniest dog slept, away from the others. Castor's brother, Runt, was lying on his back in full sun with the soft part of his stomach exposed. The pavement beneath him had to be scalding.

"You bit me," Alpha said in disbelief. He stepped forward, casting a menacing shadow over the sleeping dog. Runt's front paws, drawn up to his chest, gave the slightest twitch, but he didn't wake.

Bit. Castor licked his chops. Hadn't he just been biting into something? He could almost taste the meat, and a faint metallic tang of blood was on his tongue and in the air. He followed the scent, his nose twitching with the awful realization that it wasn't a deer's leg he'd sunk his teeth into; it was Alpha's.

And Runt was already taking the heat for it. Again.

"You. Bit. Me." Now Alpha's growl was a guttural threat.

Runt's eyes opened, red-rimmed and still cloudy with sleep. Runt didn't seem to grasp the vulnerability of his situation. Instead of jumping to attention, he yawned and stretched his skinny legs in the air.

Alpha was practically foaming at the mouth, and if Castor hadn't lunged forward when he did, the bigger dog would've torn Runt in two.

"It was me," Castor said quickly, shoving his body between them. He whined a little and wagged his tail to show he meant peace.

Alpha wasn't buying it, though. The boxer's stubby ears lay back against his broad, white head. "Stay out of it," he snarled at Castor, his lips curling to expose pink gums and sharp canines.

Castor bared his own teeth, but then thought better of it. He was no coward—he'd often held his own in street brawls with other packs of dogs. But with Alpha, power was always an act, and Castor was smart enough to know when to play along. Of course Alpha knew it was Castor who hunted in his sleep—the whole pack knew—but that wasn't the point. Alpha tormented Runt because Runt was the omega, and that's how things worked.

"Didn't mean to interrupt," Castor apologized, though he didn't budge. "What were you saying, Alpha?" Finally alert, Runt cowered behind his brother, peering through Castor's legs as he waited for his leader to deliver punishment.

Alpha puffed out his muscled chest and jutted his underbite forward. "This pathetic excuse for a canine was about to tell me what happens when you offend Alpha."

"Scavenge," Runt panted from the ground, his chest quivering. "No pack."

Castor's ears pricked up. Despite the risks, he loved solo scavenging missions—for once he could really rely on his instincts, run fast without hanging back for the group, feel the air rustling his fur and the muscles in his legs working to a sweaty lather. He could help his brother out and get a taste of freedom; he just had to convince Alpha to "punish" him, too.

Humiliating as it was, Castor made himself bow his head and curl his tail under his legs. Then he made a big show of crawling toward Alpha, keeping his belly low to the ground. "I could go with Runt," he suggested in his meekest bark, casting his eyes down. And before Alpha could growl a refusal, Castor quickly added, "We might even be able to hunt. . . ."

"As if you two morons would know prey from your own legs," Alpha scoffed. "Or mine," he added pointedly. But Castor heard the drips splatter on the pavement, and he didn't have to look up to know Alpha was salivating.

The pack had been living on garbage for weeks. It had once been easy to find vermin hiding in the trash mountains on the outskirts of the city, but now that they were crawling with Crusher Slusher machines, grinding down decades worth of the humans' discarded toys, the dogs had to make due with rotten scraps along the edges. The pack was getting restless.

Alpha might not think much of Runt, but despite the omega dog's cowardice and slight build, he was still from

4

the same litter as Castor. They had the same shaggy fur, same black muzzles of their German shepherd mother, with a dash of boldness she'd insisted came from their Mexican wolf side. And together, even Alpha had to admit, the brothers could hunt.

"Go," the pack leader finally said with a dismissive toss of his head.

Castor licked Alpha's chin to show respect, but he turned too quickly, betraying his giddiness. He felt a sharp pain as Alpha snapped at his hind leg. "And don't come back without some fresh meat, you hear me?"

2

THE BROTHERS RAN TOGETHER, MATCHING STEP FOR STEP, breath for breath. The farther they went into the city, the taller and more packed together the black glass towers grew. The domed walkways that ran between them crisscrossed until they blocked out every last bit of sun. It was never dark, though—every side of every building flashed dozens of lifelike images each minute: political nonsense and Lion's Head news. Pictures selling things that glittered and things that glowed and things that promised to change your life. Humans like you never saw them in real life—with faces three stories tall instead of tiny dots, sitting outside, grinning up at the sun with exposed pink and brown flesh, looking like they weren't afraid of all the things crawling up their upturned noses through the air.

Over the years, Castor had taught himself to read by staring at those changing pictures. It was a useless hobby and one he never would've admitted to in front of Alpha, but Runt got a kick out of hearing about the strange human world, and he was constantly bugging Castor for updates.

Or he usually was. Apart from the sound of their panting, Runt was suspiciously quiet. Runt was never quiet.

Castor noticed that Runt's tail was tucked between his legs. "You scared?" he asked his brother.

"I just don't like being separated from the pack this far in."

"If we run into Chauncy Chow, I've got your back like always," Castor promised, scanning the narrow alleyways between the factories for their territory rivals.

"I don't care about Chauncy or his wee weenies," Runt scoffed. "They're just fancy rodents."

Castor barked a laugh. It was true. Humans had bred

miniature breeds when space was tight, but now that virtual pets were in fashion, the pampered minis were being dumped on the streets, too. The so-called "rival pack" was a whiny group of dachshunds led by an entitled puffball.

"Then what?" Castor asked. "Is it the Crusher Slushers?" They'd seen a street scrubber suck up one of Chauncy's weenies just last week. The mini dog disappeared into the big iron shell, and there was a grind of gears, and then a slurp, and the only thing the Crusher left behind was a slushy liquid that oozed into the gutter. He knew Runt was still pretty shaken up about it.

"No," Runt said. "I know we can outrun them. But aren't you worried about the humans?" His eyes darted around as if one might pop out at any moment. "The Gray Whiskers always say they're the biggest threat of all."

"Those old-timers haven't been in the streets since way back before the sun sickness," Castor said dismissively. When Runt didn't respond, Castor stopped running and turned to his brother. "Runt, have you ever seen a human in your entire life?" he asked seriously.

"There's a bunch of them right up there." Runt tilted his chin toward the clouds, where boxes suspended on strings zigzagged between the buildings. There were men inside each one, no doubt, but from here they were little more than shadows.

"Right," Castor said. "Up there. They spend their lives behind thick glass. They can't handle dust or heat or raw food. Look at them, those tiny things filing across the walkways—they're no bigger than ants!"

Runt nodded, but his tail didn't resume its usual speedy wag. He was still staring up at the building, but an advertisement had materialized on the glass walls, each word several stories high.

"'Don't miss the Mega Monster Mash-up *tonight*!'" Castor read the scrolling text. "'Warp in to watch the final face-off between this season's *murderous mutants*!!!'" He looked at Runt. "That's the competition you like, right?" An image showing a cat's huge white-and-black-striped face replaced the text. "Is that one of the gladiators?"

"Not gladiators," Runt sighed. "Unnaturals. That's the Invincible."

Pale blue eyes moved inside the big cat's face, like it was tracking them. It was too bright, too animated. It almost seemed like it might jump right out of the glass. A translucent, barbed tail arced over the head. Castor had never seen anything like that tail on the streets, but the sight of it made him shiver.

"I bet he's not afraid of the humans," Castor said.

"The Invincible? Afraid? No way!" Runt shook his head vigorously. "He wins every single match! He's a *hero*!" Runt was getting animated now. It seemed like he was back to his old self, but then he added quietly, "I bet no one tries to bully him. I bet he doesn't cower from any alpha."

"Sorry you took the blame back there," Castor offered guiltily. "I didn't mean to . . . And I tried to tell him . . ."

"It's okay." Runt cocked his head at Castor, his ears flopping sideways. "Just wish I had the guts to . . . bark back every once in a while, you know?"

Castor raised a furry eyebrow and shouldered against him playfully. "You bark more than any mutt I know, even those yipping minis!"

Runt grinned and nipped at Castor's ear, and soon his tail and his tongue were both going at top speed again. "So you were dreaming about the Greenplains again, huh? What was it like?" The smaller dog circled him excitedly, his eyes bright. He loved hearing about the Greenplains even more than the Unnaturals competitions.

"It's not like I've actually been there any more than you have," Castor said. "They're just dreams."

"The Greenplains are real!" Runt insisted. "The Gray Whiskers say so! Now tell me, tell me, tell me." He jumped and nudged. "Were there hills or streams or animals? Were there alphas? What was it like?"

Castor eyed the gray landscape that stretched before him, coated in its fine film of chemical dust. "Different from this. Greener." When Runt rolled his eyes, he added, "And the hunting was better."

In Lion's Head, Castor had never even seen a deer, let alone tasted one. He'd only ever heard of deer from the Gray Whiskers. The only prey these littered streets had in abundance were rats—small, sneaky things that would scrunch up their faces to taunt you, their beady eyes glowing red in the shadows. Castor sniffed at a drain—sometimes the more clever rats hid in there—but there was only sludge.

"Much better," he muttered. "Speaking of hunting, we should get going."

When he looked up from the drain, something else had caught Runt's attention. His tail was rigid, and his stare was trained on a shuddering pipe.

Castor's tongue darted out to lick his snout. "Is that what I think it is?"

"Raccoooon!" Runt howled, his feet tangling as he tore after it, forgetting all his fears.

3

TODAY WAS THE LUCKIEST OF DAYS. CASTOR SHOT AFTER Runt, knowing that where there was one raccoon, there were a dozen. Sure enough, though the raccoon disappeared between buildings and under garbage, each time they scared it up again, there were a few more of its little friends in their dark face masks. Castor had dreamt of meat, and now they would have a real feast.

They just had to wear them out first. Raccoons were a bit trickier to hunt than rats or squirrels. The sly little thieves were pretty scrappy in a fight, and if they weren't good and exhausted by the time you cornered them, you risked a flank full of holes from their razor teeth. Together, he and Runt tried to corral the critters into a narrower path, but it was tough without the whole pack. The raccoons kept turning and scattering, and it wasn't long before the dogs were on unfamiliar ground.

"We should turn back!" Castor called ahead to Runt.

"No way!" the usually meek omega answered, tongue wagging as he ran. "The Invincible wouldn't turn back! Laringo wouldn't be afraid!"

They were deep in enemy territory, far from their pack's markings. Castor couldn't even smell Chauncy and the wee weenies anymore, and the markings he could smell made him nervous.

"Got one!" Runt called suddenly.

Now the smell of raccoon was the brightest scent of all. Castor's stomach growled, and he felt almost delirious with hunger. Runt was right: just a little while longer, and they would have the rest of them! They were so close.

His legs carried him faster, farther, and finally, he was closing in on a group of raccoons. By the time he noticed the streaking shape of the enemy beagle in his peripheral vision, Runt was far ahead of him.

The beagle pressed toward Castor, its ears flopping

in the wind. Castor knew he could beat the smaller dog but didn't want a fight if he could avoid it. He nipped at one long ear in warning.

But the beagle wasn't backing down. His snarls told Castor he would show no mercy, and Castor's hesitation had cost him dearly: a skinny greyhound and a vicious dalmatian had joined the beagle, and together, they were closing in on him.

As a last-ditch effort, Castor took a sharp pivot and shouldered against the beagle. The force and his hefty weight caught the smaller dog off guard and sent it hurtling into both the greyhound and the spotted hothead. They all careened sideways, a jumble of limbs and tails.

"Yes!" Castor howled gleefully, shocked at his success. Now all he had to do was catch up with Runt and find a way home!

But looking ahead, Castor saw that Runt was barreling down a hill. And downhill led to a place Castor had been forbidden from puppyhood to ever, ever approach: it led to the river.

The river wasn't even water. It was muck. Swirling brown acid, where nothing survived except pink rats whose fur had been burned away, along with half their brains.

14

"Runt!" Castor barked a frantic warning. "Runt, *stop!*"

Knowing he should turn around, Castor surged forward, desperate to catch up with his brother. He called Runt's name over and over, but Runt didn't hear him, couldn't focus on anything except the fat raccoons luring him toward them. He was wild with the hunger of the hunt. Castor watched as Runt ran to the end of the road.

And right out to the end of the dock.

When Castor finally reached him, Runt was panting giddily, surrounded by four fat raccoon meals, which he began eating with his usual fervor.

"Runt," Castor said pleadingly, the toxic smell of the river burning in his throat. "We need to go. Now."

"I got 'em!" Run grinned around a mouthful of raccoon fur. "I told you I'd get 'em!"

"And we got you," a voice barked from behind them.

Castor whirled around. It was the beagle's voice, but the dalmatian and the greyhound were there, too . . . along with eleven more of their friends. The entire rival pack was lined up, blocking their exit.

"Ohhh no," Runt whimpered when he saw the other dogs. The limp raccoon fell from his jaws.

"Oh yes," the beagle said. His ear was still bleeding.

"On this side of town, we don't take kindly to Southside mutts stealing our meat."

"On this side of town," the dalmatian said, his pale eyes unblinking, "meat is so scarce we sometimes feast on enemy dog."

Runt couldn't help it—he let out a submissive whine. The other dogs laughed.

"Runt, get behind me," Castor commanded in a low, cautious growl. Then he lowered his head. He would fight every last one of them before they could touch his brother. "Come at me," he growled at the rival pack, his lips twitching over his fangs.

And come they did. They were muscled or skinny, long-haired or short; they were all vicious. The dock was narrow, so he only had to fight two or three at a time, but the next group was always ready. Castor felt teeth sinking into his belly, snapping at his legs. Gnawing on his tail like an old bone. The beagle whose ear he'd nipped got revenge by biting one of Castor's ears down the middle.

Within minutes, Castor seemed to be hurting from everywhere at once, and every inch of his body quivered in agony. Still, he fought back with a fierceness he never knew was in him. He bulldozed into the foe, snarling as he lunged. He shouldered a husky off the dock, and though he heard the splash, the next dog was already on

16

him before he could look toward the river.

He had to get one more bite in, disable one more dog. He only wanted to save his brother, and maybe survive while he was at it. He knew he probably didn't have a chance, but at least he'd go out with honor.

Then, all of a sudden, the other dogs were scrambling away. One after another, with their ears flat against their skulls and their eyes wide with fear, they turned tail and fled. Were they afraid of the river after what had happened to the husky? Or had Castor actually managed to win?

"We're okay," Castor said, still bewildered. He was bleeding and limping, and he could feel the painful tear in his right ear where the beagle had latched on, but they were both alive.

"We're better than okay." Runt scooted toward Castor, gratefully licking at his ears and cheeks. "I can't believe you took on that whole pack!"

"Maybe I should challenge Alpha," Castor joked, feeling proud despite himself. Runt frowned. "Or not . . . I mean, I was kidding."

But Runt wasn't looking at him. His usually floppy ears were standing up, alert, and he let out a fearful growl.

"What?" Castor asked, confused. He heard nothing.

Runt scrambled to his feet now, and there was no trace of the joy that had been on his face moments before. "Is that . . . ?"

Then Castor heard it. His ear must've been damaged worse than he thought, because the noise was close now—too close—and it made every hair on Castor's coat stiffen.

It was a crushing sound—like bones being ground up—and then a slurp.

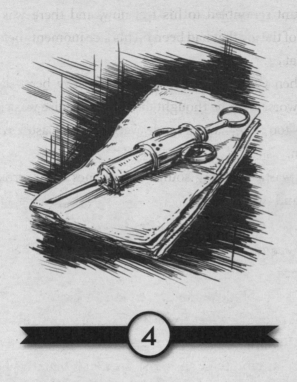

4

CASTOR LOOKED UP THE HILL TO SEE THE SNAILLIKE machine with the words WASTE MANAGEMENT stamped on it. Then the Crusher Slusher was hurtling toward them, giant and menacing, and before Castor and Runt could reach the start of the dock, it was already blocked off.

Near the Crusher, they could see the dust and debris trembling on the pavement. Then Castor saw the raccoons' fur rustling, and he could feel the high-force suction starting to pull at him. He and Runt scrabbled at the wood planks of the dock, desperately trying to find purchase.

Castor bared his teeth, and the loose skin of his jowls pulled away from his face. The wind was so strong now that it dried his eyes, making everything blurry. As he was dragged blindly toward the awful gears, Castor couldn't believe that, after everything he'd survived in his scrappy life, this was the end. He almost wished the dogs had torn him apart instead.

Abruptly, the sound cut out. The Crusher had stopped.

Castor blinked rapidly, trying to clear his vision. Runt, only a few feet from the machine now, turned to look at him, wide-eyed. Castor stepped forward and peered around the Crusher Slusher with tentative hope. If it had died, they could squeeze around it. . . .

A figure in orange stepped out of the top of the Crusher, and Castor froze. Runt's eyes went wider and white with terror, and Castor knew he could never make up for how wrong he'd been, how stupidly reassuring, how confident.

It was a human.

Not a faraway figure trapped behind glass. This was a human on the street, standing in front of him. At least that's what he thought it was.

Castor had thought humans looked like the faces he'd seen in the virtual posters, but this creature looked almost insect-like. Its face was greenish, and it had large, round, tinted eyes, like those he'd seen on flies. It seemed to have trouble breathing—he could hear its labored breaths coming out of its weird circular mouth—and it was covered in billowing orange fabric and gloves— probably to hide the rest of its hideous skin.

It was terrifying, and it was lumbering toward him.

Castor didn't know what to do, so he studied it like prey or an enemy dog. He noted the vulnerable parts— the fleshy sides, the fingers, the unstable two-legged balance.

Get away, he barked at the human.

The creature hesitated and turned its head, and for a moment, Castor thought his warning had worked and it was about to retreat. But instead, another human was moving in on them.

"What do you have there?" the second one called.

"Just a couple of mutts," the first answered over its shoulder. "I tried to suck 'em up, but the old clunker's not what she used to be." It reached one of its orange arms toward the Crusher Slusher and rapped against the metal. "Careful," it said as the second human stepped

21

toward Castor. "That one's vicious. Just saw him take on a dozen other dogs in a fight."

"Really?" The human cocked its head but continued forward anyway, and Castor saw that it was holding something in its hands. Something hard and dark and mean-looking. Something that seemed familiar somehow, that Castor might've seen on one of the flashing pictures at some point. . . . The human brought it up to its face, peering through its hard, reflective eyes.

Castor snarled, crouching back on his haunches. But before he could so much as spring, a whirr echoed in his ears, and Castor was suddenly on the ground, bewildered at the failure of his muscles. A piece of colored plastic was poking out of his flank, Castor noticed with alarm. He'd been shot!

Runt whined and licked at him, distraught. "What is it, what is it, can I kill it?" he panted.

Castor didn't have time to think about that now, though—his senses felt off. There seemed to be twice as many men, their orange outlines blurring every time he blinked, and Runt looked like he was glowing strangely. When the men spoke, their voices were hollow and muffled.

"What'd you do that for?" The first man's hazy form stepped forward.

"You know NuFormz, the warehouse on the island, where the old prison used to be? I got a buddy over there, Slim, who says they're looking for a fresh crop of animals for that Mega Media reality show—*Unnaturals*, or whatever. I bet those lab coats will pay a pretty penny for a prize like this."

"I'd sure put my money on 'im in the ring," the other agreed. "I love a good match."

Castor's mind was racing. He'd heard of dog disappearances before. Was this what had happened to his great-uncle Carmine or to the collie mutt last year? Had the Gray Whiskers' warnings been right all along?

He struggled to his feet, or rather he scuttled sideways like a spider, tripping over his own paws. His legs weren't working right. They were heavy and felt like they were made of the brown sludge in the river—all liquidy.

"Come on, then," the man with the weapon said, his voice echoing. "I'll give you a cut of the cash if you help me get him in my truck." Their bodies seemed to flicker as they stepped toward Castor.

Now it was Runt's turn to defend his brother. He stood in front of him, and his frantic barking was an alarm for every animal within earshot.

"Easy, there," one of the men said, gesturing for Runt to move aside. "It's not you we want."

Castor was proud when Runt responded with a snarl and a snap of his jaws, but then they shot him with the poison arrow, too.

Castor's head felt so heavy now that he couldn't even protest as the insect men lifted him with their gloved hands and threw him into a cage in the back of a truck. The bars crossed in front of him and he smashed his face into them, scratching his nose.

Runt started to howl now, and even after the doors of the truck closed and the metal box started to move, Castor could hear his brother's voice—a long, mournful wail of protest. It trailed them for miles, until Castor lost consciousness.

5

Across the river and 247 stories up, Marcus was in his bedroom, listening to music on full blast and practicing kick flips on his skateboard as he scanned the simulink network for updated stats on the Unnaturals, like he did before every match.

He was only allowed to watch four of the sixteen fights each season, because his stepdad, Bruce the Brutal, worried about "overexposure to violence." That was totally uncool, considering he was eleven years

old—only fifteen months away from being a teenager!—
but it was also totally hypocritical. Not only did
Bruce help Marcus's older brother, Pete, get a job with
NuFormz, but Bruce helped design the monsters, which
he'd confided to Marcus were only virtual models,
anyway. But like any die-hard fan, Marcus still knew
the mutants' histories by heart, especially the ones on
his favorite team.

Team Scratch had had a rough time lately. That was
putting it mildly; the Invincible had led Team Klaw on
a five-season winning streak, and he wasn't showing
any sign of slowing down. Pookie the Poisonous—the
Chihuahua-spider—was the only one that could hold a
candle to the scorpion-tiger, and he'd been mysteriously
retired halfway through last season. Then the Crunch,
a cockroach-crocodile that everyone thought would be
super tough, had gotten squashed in his first match,
bankrupting half the gamblers in Lion's Head. Things
had just gone downhill from there, and almost every
time Marcus had checked the simulink, at least one
member of Team Scratch was listed as injured.

Still, Marcus wasn't giving up hope. Tonight was the
final showdown, the Mega Monster Mash-up, when all
the creatures fought at once. It was the most important
match of the season, the only match that really counted,

and Marcus had a warp ticket with his name on it.

He scanned the stats projected in front of his eyes. Even as a loyal Scratch fan, he knew it didn't look good. Team Klaw's odds were 62:1.

There was a flicker of movement in his peripheral vision, and Marcus looked away from the simulink toward the floor-to-ceiling warp screen on the far wall of his room. He could see Matchmaker Joni Juniper—or her avatar, at least—descending from the ceiling of the Dome in the mouth of a golden lion. As she reached the center space next to the scoreboard, the lion roared and erupted in an explosion of stars that turned into a banner.

MEGA MEDIA PRESENTS:
UNNATURALS FINAL FACE-OFF!

"The match is starting!" Marcus called downstairs to his mother.

The Matchmaker's mouth was moving. Marcus killed the guitar-shredding noise of Sky Seizure and popped in his magni-sound earbuds.

"The time has come," she announced. "For the night all you Moniacs have been waiting for! The Mega! Monster! Mash-up!"

Marcus usually hated that lame fanboy term, *Moniac*,

but Joni Juniper was a total skyrocket, with honey-brown skin and a cloud of soft, dark auburn ringlets that framed her face, and when she said it, he actually blushed. He felt way too far away from the stadium, though—it was time to warp!

"Mom?" he called again, pulling out one of the earbuds. "Ticket code? Pleeease?"

"Sure, sweetie," his mom answered. "As soon as you finish your history homework."

Uh-oh.

"Who cares about the Warming Age?" Marcus groaned. He'd been procrastinating on this research feed all day. What was the point of reading about the animals that went extinct in the past, when you could watch newer, cooler virtual animals fight right now?

When his mom didn't answer, Marcus sighed and turned back to the simulink and pulled up the list his teacher had generated, scanning it for something he recognized. Aha: hippopotamus! He thought he knew enough about a former Unnatural, a Komodo dragon–hippo mix, to whip up a quick feed. He remembered the Hellion's crazy-powerful jaw, and that gross red drool, and started dictating the text.

"The hippo's teeth sharpened themselves when ground together, and by overproducing saliva to slick things up, they could swallow their enemies whole."

Or was that the lizard half of it? Marcus wasn't sure, but he was able to bluff his way through a mediocre couple of pages, and soon enough he'd uploaded it to the school's inter-verse. "Mom!" he screamed desperately. "Finished!"

The simulink beeped and moments later, the ticket code materialized in front of his face. Marcus popped the earbuds back in, slid the Blink over his eye, and pulled his desk chair up close to the warp screen. When his fingers made contact with the filmy material, a numerical key appeared, he tapped out the code, and a cartoon lion breaking his chains appeared on-screen, confirming his entry.

Warp time, baby!

The Blink clicked on and Marcus felt slightly dizzy as his eyes adjusted to the 4D image on the screen. Then he was there.

Or he was as much there as you could be without actually having tickets to the live match. Marcus knew he was still in his bedroom, of course, but other than the feel of the chair cushion beneath him, it sure seemed like he was in the Dome. When he rotated in his chair, his view expanded to a 360-degree view of the inside of the stadium. He saw the metallic sheen of the curved ceiling, the hologram of Joni Juniper dancing through the air as she revved up the crowd, and the crowd itself, thousands of people in the sloping bleachers all around him. They looked angry.

Marcus gave a voice command to crank up the volume on his earbuds, and the sound of booing rushed into his ears.

He looked down toward the wide, dusty circle at the center of the Dome. The Invincible was prowling around the arena, looking more terrifying than ever. His imposing white tiger's body rippled with muscle, razor-like teeth glinted under the Dome's bright lights in a permanent snarl, and a long scorpion's tail curved over his head.

It looked like that stinger had done some serious damage; in the ten minutes it had taken Marcus to finish his homework, the match was already over, and with it, the season.

Looking around the arena at the aftermath of the Invincible's rampage, Marcus was sick to his stomach. He tore off his Blink and warped out of the stadium, feeling cheated. He tossed his earbuds on the bed and joined his mom in the kitchen.

She was furiously chopping vegetables and dumping them in a pan, and Marcus peered around her arms to get a look at what she was cooking.

"Honey, don't touch," his mom said. "Bruce is going to be home any minute, and I've got to finish this. You know he likes his food hot when he walks in the door."

Marcus couldn't care less what Bruce the Brutal liked.

"I hate stew, anyway," he grumbled. "I'll have a Vita pill or something."

His mom made a sound of disapproval in her throat that told him that wasn't an option. "A capsule of powdered protein is not sufficient for a growing boy." Then she glanced up from the food she was making. "Hey, I thought you were warping into the match. Is it over so soon?"

"The Invincible won again," he said, more to himself than her.

"It's just virtual reality, honey," she said, repeating what she and Bruce always like to remind him. "It's just entertainment."

Well, it hadn't been very entertaining, that was for sure. It would be almost a month before the new mutants started competing—not that it mattered much. As a Team Scratch fan, it was getting harder and harder to get excited about another season.

So much for a comeback.

6

BENEATH THE CITY OF LION'S HEAD, IN A TINY APARTMENT in the underground neighborhood known as the Drain, Leesa was hard at work on a letter. Or she would be, if she could just figure out how to start it.

She sat cross-legged on the sagging couch that doubled as her bed and hunched over the tablet in her lap, staring at the blank screen. Her hair hung around her face in a sleek dark curtain but for the one streak she'd recently dyed blue.

What did you say to a sky queen politician? What could you say that would make her listen?

Her friend Antonio would say she was an idiot for writing the letter at all, but Leesa was desperate, and Eva Eris was the only person she could think of who had any real power.

> Dear Mayor Eris,
> I need your help in a really bad situation.

Ugh, that sounded lame. If she wanted an important lady like the mayor to take her seriously, she had to sound more grown-up. Leesa deleted the line, her fingers hovering above the screen. Then she had it.

> I'm requesting your assistance with a very
> grave matter. Mega Media has gone too far with
> its Unnatural monster matches. The Mash-up
> was . . .

Brutal? Disgusting?

> The Mash-up was HORRIBLE!

The images Leesa had seen during the last fight were

a scar in her memory, and she felt the nausea over again. After that night, she'd wanted to walk away from the Unnaturals forever. She almost had.

She glanced down at the paperback she'd been reading, propped open on the cushion next to her. Leesa's teacher, Ms. Hoiles, often lent Leesa old books—really old ones, made from paper and everything—but she couldn't have known how the sight of that cover would affect Leesa. *Charlotte's Web* was spelled out in fancy letters, with a web winding around them. There was a tiny spider dangling down, and a girl smiling up at it. Looking at the image, all Leesa could think about was Pookie, her Chihuahua, and she knew it was time to finally do something. He was the reason she needed to write the letter.

The sentences flowed faster now.

Lots of kids are told that the wizards at
Mega Media create these animals from scratch.
However, I know the truth. My dog, Pookie, ran
away four years ago and was <u>accidentally</u> drafted
into the Unnaturals. They transformed him
into Pookie the Poisonous. He was retired last
season, but I still don't have him back with me.
I was hoping you could step in and—

Leesa heard someone fumbling at the front door. She glanced at the time, and a chill went through her. It was only five o'clock. Her mom didn't get off work for another two hours. Crime had been up in the Drain since the latest rationing, and Leesa lived on one of the worst streets.

The locks rattled, and Leesa gripped her tablet tightly. There was nowhere to run or hide; the whole apartment was only one room. All she could do was hold her breath as each of the eight dead bolts clicked open, one after the other.

The door burst open with a bang, and Leesa screamed.

Then she instantly felt like a baby. It was her mother. Of course it was—who else would it be?

Her mom kicked the door closed behind her. "Sorry, lovebug," she said, out of breath. "I didn't mean to burst in like that, but I was about to drop everything."

Leesa got up and maneuvered through the small, cluttered space to help her mom.

"You're home so early," Leesa said, taking two of the heaping bags. She couldn't remember her mom ever coming home from work early. "Time is money," she always said, and they never seemed to have enough of either. After a full day of running errands for rich sky dwellers too scared of pollutants to venture to ground level, her mom would crash on the couch and nap for a few hours while Leesa stayed up to read. Then, when Leesa headed to bed, her mom would take off again for the midnight shift, monitoring robots for her other job at the ReadyGro factory.

"What'd you expect?" Her mom set down her burden on the counter and tugged playfully on one of Leesa's braids. "It's your birthday, isn't it?"

Was it? Leesa blinked. She'd been so caught up in what was going on with the Unnaturals that she'd totally forgotten.

Her mom started to unload the bags, and Leesa gasped at what she saw: ReadyGro tomatoes. Broccoli. Noodles. Bottled sauces. All premium buys.

"What's all this?" she asked, trying to temper her excitement. "Stuff for one of the sky families?"

"No." Her mom's eyes shined in the dim light. "This is just for us. I thought we could sit down for a real meal together for once, to celebrate." She started putting the synthi-veggies in the fridge.

"Aw, Mom . . ." Leesa's stomach growled in antici-pation of the feast. Still, she couldn't help feeling guilty. "You didn't have to spend all that money."

They mostly lived on Vita pills these days, with the

36

occasional frozen dinner thrown in when they could afford it. Leesa had vague memories of her mom cooking meals from scratch when she was little, but since her dad had left and they'd moved to the Drain, it was completely unheard of.

Her mom waved her off. "Hush. Twelve is a big deal! My baby's almost all grown up." She tickled Leesa's sides, like she had when she was little.

"Mom, stop." Leesa rolled her eyes, but she was beaming.

"Besides, you've been so down lately, I figured you needed cheering up. I just wish I could've given you more," her mom said with a sigh. She turned away to brew her tea—with her crazy sleep schedule, Leesa's mom drank a lot of tea—but Leesa could hear the sadness in her voice. "I was really trying to save up for an automapooch for your birthday, but I just couldn't swing it this year."

"It's okay," Leesa said brightly. "I don't want a virtual pet, anyway." Wanting to reassure her mom, she walked back to the couch and grabbed the tablet. "Look." She showed her the letter she'd been writing. "When the mayor reads my petition, we're going to get Pookie back."

Her mom stared at the words, her face a mask. Then

she sank down into the couch like her legs were too wobbly to stand. "Oh, lovebug." She covered her face with her hands, obviously upset.

"What is it?" Leesa asked. Her mom was one of the toughest people she knew, and it took a lot to make her stop smiling, let alone break down.

What could be so awful about writing to the mayor?

Leesa's mom took one of Leesa's hands in both of hers and pulled her down next to her. "I didn't want to tell you this before. But maybe now that you're a little older, you can understand."

Now Leesa was alarmed. She and her mom had lived in such close quarters for so long, she didn't think they had any secrets—well, almost any. She hadn't told her mom about sneaking into the Dome with Antonio to watch Unnaturals matches all these years, but that was different. That would've worried her, and the last thing Leesa wanted was to add to her mom's worries.

Her mom looked super worried right now, though, and it was totally freaking Leesa out. She squeezed her mom's hand. "Tell me."

Instead of answering right away, Leesa's mom took Leesa's shoulders and guided them to turn. Leesa raised her eyebrows in confusion, but she obediently turned away from her mother, tucking her legs up under herself on the couch. Her mom started to comb through her hair with her fingers, like she had when Leesa was little. It felt nice, but Leesa was too anxious to enjoy it. She stared at the wall, waiting.

"Leesa, the mayor isn't going to help you get your dog back," her mom said. She separated Leesa's hair into two sections and took a deep breath. "That woman is the reason Pookie's gone."

Leesa snapped her head around. "How could it be her fault?" That didn't make any sense. "Pookie ran away. He slipped his collar like he'd done before—you always said I put it on too loose—and he went exploring and got lost on the streets and picked up by scouts and—"

"He didn't get lost, sweetie," her mom interrupted. "And the Unnaturals scouts didn't find him." Leesa caught a glimpse of the pain in her eyes before her mom signaled for her to turn back around. Her mom started to braid one of the sections of Leesa's hair, winding the strands over one another in a tight line down her head. Finally, she said in a whisper, "Your dad gave Pookie to them."

"What?" Leesa squeaked. Her dad? No. Why would he do that? And how could her mom not tell her? Nothing made sense. Feeling the tug against her scalp, she didn't dare turn back around, so she stared at a long, jagged crack on the wall as she said, "All those days I spent walking around the streets at ground level, calling for him. And all those years after, hoping he'd come back . . ."

The crack blurred.

"I know, lovebug. I'm sorry." She could hear that her mom was crying, too, and Leesa's head bobbed as the braiding got clumsier. "I didn't want you to hate your father. Your dad is a good man but a bad businessman. This all started because he wanted a better life for us. He didn't want to see you grow up in darkness, underground, didn't want to see his baby girl—" Her voice broke. "Living in a pit like this."

Leesa wiped her nose and made herself stop shaking so her mom would continue. She needed to know the whole story. "What does the mayor have to do with anything?"

"Did you know Mayor Eris was the one who started the Sky Project?"

"Everyone knows that." When Leesa was little, there was no space anywhere, and everyone was living all smashed together. Eva Eris funded research to build higher than anyone thought possible, and soon Lion's Head was thriving again—they said she'd saved the city. When she decided to run for mayor, she'd won in a landslide.

"Well, we couldn't really afford one of those fancy sky homes, but Eva told your dad we could get by on credit for a while. She had just bought this new virtual reality network, and if he offered up collateral . . ."

"Wait." Leesa sat up straighter. "So Mayor Eris owns Mega Media? She started the Unnaturals?" She couldn't believe what she was hearing.

"I think she wanted it mostly for ad propaganda. She never thought her little reality show project would take off, but when it did, she needed animals. And we were way overdue on rent."

"Pookie was the collateral." Leesa couldn't hide the bitterness in her voice. "And Dad just handed him right over."

"No, lovey." Her mom tied off the second braid and finally let Leesa turn around. "He thought it was temporary, and he tried to fix it. He really did." She took a long sip of tea and studied Leesa's face, as if deciding whether to say more. Finally, she continued, "I'm not sure if you know this, Lees, but your dad likes to gamble."

Leesa looked away. Did she know her dad gambled? Everyone in the Drain knew. He was so pathetic that not even Vince would take his bets anymore. Leesa walked to the mirror and studied her braids, tugging some hair out of the top of one of them to show off the chunk she'd dyed blue. Careful to keep a straight face, she said, "I think I might've had an idea."

Her mother looked ashamed. "He wasn't always like that. Baba went to the Dome just trying to win enough to get Pookie back. Some touts gave him inside info on who to bet on, and Baba trusted them."

Leesa winced at how easy a mark her dad had been. Even she knew not to trust the touts.

"They were all working for the mayor, of course. When he lost, Baba started placing daily double bets to try to break even again. Unfortunately, when he lost those, too, it hit us twice as hard. By the time he started winning, it was too late."

Leesa felt sick. Everything was starting to make awful, perfect sense. "That's why we moved to the Drain, isn't it? Mayor Eris got Pookie and the house?"

Her mom met her eyes and nodded, and there was something else written there between them but left unsaid: it was also why Baba didn't live with them anymore.

Leesa gripped the tablet tightly in her hands, resisting the urge to chuck it across the room only because she knew how expensive it was. So much for her letter.

"But now we're free." Her mom reached out to tuck the blue strands behind Leesa's ear. "And I'm going to keep working and keep saving, and one day, things are going to get better." Then her solemn tone changed to one of forced enthusiasm. "We're already doing pretty well for ourselves, though, aren't we? Look at this feast!" She hopped up off the couch and gave Leesa's knee a shake. "Now come on, we'd better get cooking if you want me to stay awake for your birthday dinner."

"I don't really feel like celebrating." Her family was broken and her dog was gone and everything seemed stacked against her. The only thing Leesa felt like doing was curling up and crying.

"Birthday girls aren't allowed to mope." Her mom's voice was peppy but firm. "If I've learned anything, it's that when things get hard you just have to trust in yourself, Leesa. We're stronger than we think."

That made Leesa look up, and this time, her mom held her gaze without blinking. Then she smiled.

"Probably not strong enough to blow out twelve candles at once, though!" her mom turned, unveiling what looked and smelled like a pineapple sponge cake. "I was thinking we should have dessert first, but if you're not up to it . . ."

"Okay, okay!" Leesa stood up. "Mom?" Her mom looked back at her. "I love you."

"Love you too, lovebug."

The cake was good—maybe better than anything she'd ever eaten—and it must've cost her mom a week of wages. But Leesa was most grateful for something her mom had said. Of all the things they'd talked about tonight, of all the information she'd learned, it was just three words that really stuck with Leesa: *trust in yourself.*

If she wanted something to be done about the Unnaturals, Leesa was going to have to do it on her own.

7

"I CAN'T BELIEVE SAMKEN'S GONE," A SOFT VOICE SAID
from somewhere that sounded close and far away at
once.

Castor squinted into the dim light, growling warily.
He didn't know who was speaking, and he didn't know
who Samken was; all he knew for sure was that they were
not part of his pack.

"Look, the s-s-shepherd dog's awake," another voice
hissed.

Barely. It had been a full day since they'd shot him, and Castor was still groggy. It was like that time he'd eaten the rotten rat meat, hallucinating all sorts of weird things.

Even now, he wasn't sure what was real. Outside of his cage, there were other cages, with other creatures. They smelled foreign and dangerous, and not only were they not dogs, but they were unlike anything he'd ever seen. As he looked around, he tried to remember all the different types of animals the Gray Whiskers had told him about in stories. There was a fat rope that could talk; a squat, scaled animal in a large cage on the floor—was this a lizard?—and last night he thought he'd seen a huge animal with a gray, fleshy arm for a nose. He'd always thought that the Gray Whiskers' stories about elephants were a lie until now.

For the first time in his life, Castor really understood how Runt felt; he was deep in enemy territory, and he'd never felt more vulnerable or more weak.

His bones ached all over, from the end of his tail to the tip of his wet nose, and when he tried to stand, his legs were still stiff and uncooperative. And he was so thirsty. His tongue felt huge inside his mouth, his throat too scratchy to swallow.

"Water," Castor begged. When no one answered

him, he turned around and around clumsily in the small prison of his cage, searching.

"Oh, look, it's chas-s-sing its tail," said the snake. "How s-s-special."

Then Castor saw it. There, in the next cage over, was a beautiful silver dish of water. Eagerly, Castor stuck his muzzle through the bars and drank from the bowl.

"That's *mine!*" a terrifying voice roared as a giant orange head took over Castor's vision.

Castor scrambled backward, slamming into metal bars. As much as he hated the humans, right then, he was grateful for the cage that kept him safe.

From the way the room went silent, Castor figured the giant animal to be the alpha, which he didn't quite understand because her voice was female. And worse, she seemed feline. She was like one of the alley cats that were always taunting his pack—same whiskers, same stupid stripes. But this thing was bigger. Meaner. And those teeth were no kitty cat's nibblers.

Castor watched, transfixed, as the head dipped down, its huge yellow eyes still trained on him. When she started to lap at the water bowl, Castor whined in agony, despite himself.

"You're dehydrated. It's just the sedative wearing off."

Castor spun around. The animal in the cage behind

47

his was speaking to him. It looked like some sort of rodent, but it was unlike any rat he'd ever seen. Its fur was a soft white instead of dingy gray, and its tail was no more than a puffed-up little ball. The weirdest parts were its ears. They weren't small and useless like a rat's; they were noble ears like his—long and silky and standing straight up.

Still, if it looked like a rat and smelled like a rat, it probably tasted like a rat. From the way it cowered from the other animals, Castor guessed it was probably food for the alpha and her strange pack—which meant it was off-limits. Castor felt the emptiness in his stomach, remembering the chase before he was captured.

The long-eared rat studied him for a moment with curious red eyes. "Here," she finally whispered, and then nudged her own water bowl across her cage to where he could reach it. "Have some of mine."

Castor looked up in surprise. She wanted to share her water?

After the incident with the alpha, Castor was wary. He was away from his pack, in an unfamiliar place. He knew he shouldn't trust anyone.

He shrank back into the corner of his cage, determined to resist, but the temptation was too much. Keeping an eye on the animals around him, he hunched over in the cramped space and slurped at the bowl. The water tasted sour and gritty, but it cooled his tongue and helped clear his head.

"Slow down," the white rat warned as he snuffled, spilling some of the precious liquid. "You'll make yourself sick."

She was right. Castor retched a little and saw he'd almost drunk the entire bowl. He looked up guiltily, the fur on his neck dripping. "Don't you want some?"

Her nose twitched. "I . . ."

"The poor widdle wabbit only knows how to drink from a bottle," the massive orange cat taunted.

The "wabbit" froze, her whole body quivering in terror.

"Leave her alone," Castor growled at the alpha, surprising himself. He didn't understand the pecking order of this place, but he did understand kindness. And cruelty.

"Says who? *You?*" she roared. "A scrappy dog thinks he's going to fight a royal tigress?" She hissed the last word and slammed her body forward, rattling Castor's cage.

"Alert, alert!" shrieked a colorful bird in the corner, bobbing its head. "*Alert!*"

The cat pulled back from the bars immediately, as if the bird was the alpha. "You're lucky, street dog." Her pupils dilated. "This time."

Castor shrank back farther into his cage, too. He knew he'd overstepped, but the white rat had given him water, and that was something a littermate would do— something he would've done for Runt.

"I'm Jazlyn, by the way," the long-eared rat said shyly. She nodded toward the alpha cat and whispered, "That's Enza."

"Castor," he answered, and then looked toward the bird, who seemed to have the most power. "Who's that guy?"

"Oh, that's Perry," Jazlyn said, her voice uneasy. She maneuvered her body so the bird couldn't see her face and scooted closer to the bars of Castor's cage. "But he's not one of us," she whispered. "He's a spy for the humans."

Castor stared at the bird with contempt. He had no love for winged creatures to begin with, but this one was a traitor to all animals. Perry stared right back at him from his wooden perch and made long, vaguely threatening clicking sounds with his beak.

"But over there, that's Deja, a snake from the desert," Jazlyn said. The rope creature rattled her tail in acknowledgment. "And Rainner." She glanced toward the oversized lizard on the floor. "He doesn't really like to talk."

But Castor wasn't interested in small talk, anyway—

he needed some answers. "Do you know where we are?" he asked. "Or how we get out?"

"It's called a lab," she answered. "As for getting out of here . . ." She shot Perry an anxious look. "I'll let you know when I figure it out. I've spent my whole life in places like this."

"In a cage?" Castor was horrified.

"Humans are fond of cages." Deja peeked out over her coiled body. "It makes them les-s-s afraid."

"Next question," Castor said. "Why do the humans look like bugs?"

Jazlyn looked at him, puzzled, but then her nose twitched with understanding. "Oh, you're talking about their gas masks. All humans wear them outside."

So they really did look like the advertisements Castor had seen and not large fly-faced monsters.

"I knew it," Castor said. "They're weak. They can't even breathe without help. When my pack gets here they're going to be sorry."

Jazlyn just smiled at him sadly.

"Your pack can't help you now," Rainner said, breaking his silence. "In this place, we fight alone. Some of us were born to conquer." He flicked his forked tongue at Castor through the bars of his cage. "And others are destined to fall."

8

As much as Castor wanted to ignore Rainner's ominous prediction, the lizard was right about one thing: Castor's pack didn't come. In the end, it was the humans who came for him, just like they came for everyone else.

It wasn't even dawn. It was still the dead of night, and all the animals were asleep in their cages. Castor was dreaming of the Greenplains again, yipping in his sleep, innocent as a puppy.

But as he padded through the lush forest, gloved

hands were reaching into his cage to yank Castor back to reality. He woke up howling in terror—reality was harsh.

Several dark figures stood over the street dog. Crinkly paper masks covered their mouths, making them breathe all weird, like monsters full of wind. "Ready?" one said. "Let's go."

Across the room, Perry bobbed his head excitedly. "Go! Go!" he repeated, and the bird's voice sent Castor into a panic. He squirmed away and circled the cage, desperate to get away from the humans' reaching hands.

"They're taking him! They're taking Cas-s-stor!" Deja hissed, and flicked her forked tongue.

Rainner started to rattle his broad body against his cage in agitation, and once again, Jazlyn froze, shuddering so hard she spilled her food pellets.

Only Enza the alpha tigress was calm. She just licked her paws, calmly bathing her face. Her yellow eyes followed Castor as he spun around and around in his cage, whimpering.

There was no way out.

Castor backed into a corner, trembling as the blue gloves descended on him. His captors handled him roughly, grabbing handfuls of fur and pinching his ears, and Castor realized they were pulling him out of the cage! He was more scared than he'd ever been—even more than when he'd faced the enemy pack—because with humans, he had no idea what to expect.

Would they crush him up, like the street cleaners did?

Would they put him to sleep again?

Frantic, Castor started to struggle and snarl. "Help!" he barked sharply, pitifully.

"Help!" the colorful bird mocked in a dog's yip, flapping his blue-and-yellow wings until it felt like wind was whipping through the room. "Help! Help!"

"Don't struggle," Jazlyn advised, since she'd had experience. "Just stay still or you'll make it worse."

But Castor didn't want to be like Jazlyn. He didn't want to spend his life in a cage. So he struggled as much as he possibly could. He dragged his hind legs and stiffened his front paws. He scrabbled and snarled, whined and begged.

Of course, they just poked him with another tranquilizer.

Castor felt his body go slack, and when they attached clamps to each of his legs and flipped him onto his back, the fight went out of him completely. With his belly up and legs splayed, Castor was in the most vulnerable position he could imagine. He was utterly at their mercy.

9

THE NEXT PART HAPPENED SO QUICKLY, BUT CASTOR knew the memories would haunt him for the rest of his life, the trauma of each detail burned brightly into his brain.

He imagined how he would describe it to Runt, if Castor ever saw him again, which was doubtful.

He would tell him that the light above the table had blinded him at first and then seemed to turn to dark spots, winking at him. White and moon-shaped, he didn't realize how comforting its hum had been until they'd switched it off.

Details like the way the inside of Castor's nostrils burned when the men swabbed his skin with a damp cloth.

And how slippery the examination table was beneath his paws, how he skidded and scratched at the metal.

Or how when he saw the needle, as long as a rat's rib, he thought they were going to kill him right then and there, and how afterward, for a long time, he wished they had.

And he'd remember that when they sent the serum hurtling through his system, he felt fire in his muscles and ice in his gut, and it seemed like the absolute worst thing that had ever—or could ever—happen to him.

"But really, the worst part of it came after," he would tell Runt someday. "When they left me alone."

Castor heard the door click shut and, still lying chained to the table, he felt the poison starting to work its way through him.

His mouth started to foam, like something rabid.

His whole body shuddered, hot and then cold.

His legs stiffened, splaying out to the sides.

His nails became harder and sharper and thicker,

and they pushed out from his paws, so long they began to curl under.

His back arched, the fur standing on end as the feathers started to poke through and unfurl. It felt like sharp, tiny claws were scratching, trying to push out of his shoulders. And it felt like his whole spine was snapping in half.

He wanted so many things in that moment: to shake off the white cone around his neck so he could lick at his unfamiliar body; to go back to yesterday, a day he had hated, when he was just a dog in a cage; to be a puppy again, snuggling against his mother. He wanted his pack and his brother and his scrappy street life.

But more than anything, Castor wanted someone to turn on the light. He was so afraid, alone in the dark.

10

"THERE'S A GOOD DOG," A MAN'S VOICE SAID AS HE BENT Castor's ears back and forced a collar over his head. Never in all of his days did Castor imagine he'd be seen in a collar, but he was still too weak to fight it.

In fact, he didn't dare move much. With unfamiliar body parts protruding in weird places, it was all Castor could do to stand steady on the table.

The man leaned over him and smiled. As he listened to Castor's heartbeat and checked his ears and shined a flashlight in his eyes, Castor studied him. It was the first human Castor had seen without a mask. Up close, the man's skin looked as pink and soft as a new puppy's; it made him seem young, but from the sparse hairs of tawny fur stubbling the bottom of his face along his chin and cheeks, Castor decided he must be a full-grown human. He wore glass circles on either side of his nose, and when he bent forward, Castor saw his own scared eyes reflected in them.

As the man gathered up Castor's body into his arms, the bandages on his back pulled and stretched, feathers crunched, and Castor whimpered. The man set him down, and Castor heard the snap of a metal clip connecting with his collar. "It's okay, boy," the man soothed.

It wasn't okay, though, and the man's gentle tone felt almost cruel after what Castor had been through. Castor bayed louder in distress.

It wasn't just the way his head swam with the medicine. It wasn't just that his footpads were especially tender or that his shoulders ached or that his usually strong stomach was clenched against waves of nausea. It wasn't even the collar strangling his throat. It was something far more basic: Castor didn't feel like himself anymore.

How could he? Just look what they'd done to him.

Look at these wings!

"All right, let's go," the man commanded, giving the leash a short tug.

With the first step Castor took, his legs slipped and sprawled in four directions and his snout slammed hard against the floor. He didn't know how to walk with these new long talons sprouting out of his toes or how to balance the heaviness of the feathered appendages that now weighed down his back.

Sighing, the man helped Castor back up and opened the door, pulling Castor behind him.

In the hallway, instead of the wide, gray sky Castor was used to seeing above him, a low ceiling pressed down, lit by long tubes of light, and cold air made the skin on his tummy pimple with bumps. He was being led somewhere new. Castor considered making a break for it. He could bite the man, or bolt through his legs. He could just run away, the metal leash clattering behind him!

But each way he looked, there were white walls, boxing everything in, and locked doors that led to who knew where. Then there was the humiliating cone around his head, and the collar around his neck that said he belonged to someone. Even if he knew how to escape, even if he could actually make this foreign body of his run all the way back to his territory and his pack, Castor wasn't sure they would accept him anymore.

He couldn't go home, not until he figured out how to return to how he was. So instead, he followed the man's jingling keys and the squeak of his rubber shoes and started the long, awkward march to wherever it was he was supposed to live now.

The place was a fortress. The man led him through a series of heavy, glass doors—Castor lost count of how many—and each time, Castor felt a small twitch of a charge inside his neck collar, and from somewhere he couldn't see, a woman said, "Processing." Castor was certain he'd never find his way out again. The only thing to do was go forward.

Finally, they passed through the last door into a large, square room. There were clear doors all around the space, and each one led to a smaller room you could see inside. The ceiling was much higher than in the hallways—as tall as some of the buildings in Lion's Head—and Castor could see each floor leading up to it had the same layout, with the glass doors running along the outside walls. Behind each one of those glass doors, on every floor, was a captured animal.

Creatures with spots, and scales, and stingers peered down from the upper levels as the man led Castor across the length of the ground floor. Their eyes were haunted, their postures cowed, but they looked whole and unchanged—not a mash-up of parts, like Castor. They weren't making any sounds, but he could smell their fear. It hung in the air and stuck in his nose.

What was this place?

"Come on, boy."

Castor hadn't realized he'd stopped until the man tugged harder on the metal chain, bunching the skin at his throat. His tail disappeared between his legs, but he made himself move forward. They walked along one wall, and Castor peered into the rooms as they passed, but they were all empty. He was the only animal on this floor.

Finally, the man stopped in front of an empty cell at the end. When the glass door slid open, Castor didn't even have it in him to put up a fight. He stepped inside.

The man followed, sliding the glass door shut behind him. Then he knelt down next to Castor and unclipped the leash from his throat. He wound it up and clipped it to his belt, and then he carefully removed Castor's plastic cone. "You should be okay without this now," he said. "Just don't lick, okay, boy?"

Castor stared at the floor, shaking all over as he waited for the human to leave. The man stayed in his crouched position, though, hesitating.

"Maybe this doesn't need to be quite so tight," he

said, testing the collar. He chewed the skin of his lips.

No, it doesn't! Castor whined, pleading with his eyes.

The man looked back at him with something like pity and started to reach for the buckle on the collar.

"What's going on in there?" another voice snapped. Through the glass, Castor saw a man rushing down the hall toward them.

"N-n-nothing," the man next to Castor stammered as he scrambled to his feet.

"Peter! You're not supposed to be in the cells!" The other man stopped outside Castor's little room and rapped on the glass urgently. Castor noticed he had one of those paper masks dangling from his neck.

And a familiar blue-and-yellow bird bobbing on his shoulder.

Castor wasn't one to hold a grudge, but when Perry fixed him with his white, unblinking traitor's stare and said, "Help! Help!" in a perfect imitation of a dog's howl, Castor couldn't help but grumble a little.

"It's fine," the man called Peter insisted. He grabbed the leash and opened the door, quickly stepping through.

"It's not fine!" the man with the blue mask scolded as he yanked the door closed behind Peter. He was older, Castor saw—he had the gray-and-white streaks around his temples that you saw in dogs that were past their prime. "Listen to him—he's growling!"

Both men peered through the glass at Castor, whose hackles were still up. He couldn't help it—he was anxious and scared, and the yelling wasn't helping.

"He's just freaked out about that stupid, squawking parrot," Peter muttered.

"Freak out!" Perry crowed for emphasis. "Freak!" he repeated, looking right at Castor.

Castor barked at the bird, and the older man glared at Peter pointedly. "You think I need a lawsuit on my hands? These creatures are designed to fight. Have you forgotten about the damage the Invincible did in the last match?"

The Invincible . . . Castor thought, his head still groggy. Where had he heard that name before?

"I know, Bruce." Peter sighed. His forehead was getting shiny. "The dog was just scared, and I—"

"He's not a dog!" the older man's shrill voice rose. "Just like you're not a handler. You're a medic, and I told your mother I didn't think you were even ready for that much responsibility. I stuck my neck out for you, Peter." He pointed a finger in warning. "Now get the cell locked up before that monster kills us both."

Monster? Castor looked at them. Was that what he was now?

Peter was fumbling for the keys in his pocket. His eyes met Castor's through the glass, and Castor stared back defiantly, daring him to do what was right.

But despite his apologetic look, the man still slid the key into the lock. He was no different from the rest of the humans, after all.

Long after he'd stopped hearing the jingle of keys and the squeak of sneakers, the click of the dead bolt echoed inside Castor's eardrums, along with Perry's mocking cry: "Freak! Freak! Freak!"

11

CASTOR HAD NO IDEA HOW LONG HE'D BEEN IN THE CELL. Time was funny here; instead of the sun's slow progress, there were artificial lights that crackled brightly no matter the time of day.

He'd passed out for a while when he was still medicated, but once the sedative wore off, he woke full of nervous energy. Castor wasn't used to being cooped up. He paced the room, not that there was any point—the rough concrete floor snagged his talons with every step, and there was absolutely nowhere to go. The cell was a small cube of space, with the thick glass door he'd entered through and three gray walls pressing in on him. The back wall looked slightly different from the others, with four square doors set into it.

Castor was definitely curious about those doors, since they seemed like his best chance of getting out of here. But none of them budged when he pushed his weight against them, so after a few hours spent futilely scratching at their edges, he lost interest.

The only other features in his new home were a straw-covered grate that he absolutely refused to go to the bathroom on, and a sorry-looking blue cushion. No food that he could smell. And no water.

Castor turned his attention to the space outside his cell, but what he saw through the glass wasn't much more exciting. All around him were empty rooms and eerie silence. He could no longer see the upper floors, but he remembered the animals he'd seen on his way in.

"Hey!" he called out to them. "Can anybody hear me?"

Castor waited, but the only reply was the echo of his own bark. The smell was still there, though—the stench of fear hung thick in the air.

Defeated, Castor plopped back down on the bed and

groaned—it was so limp that he could feel his bones pressing into the concrete. He tried to fall back asleep, but it was tough without the hum of the city or the warmth of his pack. Between the pain and the fear and the artificial light, there was no way he was going to get any rest.

Castor tried to roll over to get more comfortable, but the protrusion of his new wings made lying on his back even more awkward. But looking up for that brief moment, he saw it.

Near the ceiling of his cell, there was a wooden perch that jutted out of the wall. And on that perch, at least fifteen feet off the ground, sat a water dish.

What was it doing up there?

Castor scrambled to his feet, his eyes locked on the dish. He licked his parched lips and walked in a few circles, puzzling out how he could reach it. He stood on his hind legs and leaned against the wall. He even tried to jump a few times. Then, he had a revelation: *You're a mutant now, Castor! You can fly!*

But of course he couldn't fly. Simply having feathers didn't make you a bird, and after a few painful, frantic flaps of his wings, it was pretty clear they were more for decoration. It was just another one of the humans' cruel tricks. He'd never be able to reach that water. Ignoring the useless cushion this time, Castor sprawled out on the cold floor and heaved a great sigh.

"Gibbing up tho thoon?" a saliva-soaked voice asked.

Castor looked up. His cell was in a corner, and from this angle, he could see the first three rooms along the perpendicular wall, but he hadn't seen anyone in them. And he hadn't realized anyone could see him.

He stood up and peered through the glass into the cell closest to his, just around the corner. The room looked identical to his own, but from this angle, the back corner of it was concealed in darkness.

"Hello?" he barked. "Who's there?"

"*Me!*" Two glowing, yellow eyes snapped open in the darkness, and when the beast stepped forward into the light, Castor instinctually stepped back, despite the glass that separated them.

She was monstrous. Even standing on all fours, his neighbor was almost as tall as the humans, with a hulking body that seemed to fill up her whole cell.

"Looks like water juth ithn't your thing, huh, Cathtor?" Her eyes turned to slits as she smiled, and two thick, white tusks of bone curved down over her lips.

Castor flattened his ears, suspicious. "How do you know my name?"

"You don't recognithe me?" she asked. She paraded

back and forth behind the glass, amused. He didn't recognize that furry, brown face, not at all, but Castor's eyes lit on the long, switching tail. It was orange. And though her speech was made clumsy by those new tusks, Castor realized he recognized the velvety voice, too—a threatening purr. Castor's eyes widened. "You're . . ."

"Enza."

The alpha female from that first day. The large, striped cat. Castor could hardly believe it.

"You look so . . . different," Castor marveled.

She stalked the cell like a tiger would, and those golden eyes with their diamond-shaped pupils were definitely feline. But her stripes were gone, and her fur was now a coarse medium brown that barely verged on orange near her hindquarters.

"What'th that thuppothed to mean?" Enza's bear face hissed.

"Nothing," Castor said quickly. "I just meant your fangs."

Enza rolled her shoulders back and pressed her felted pink tongue against her incisors. "Saber teeth," she corrected, and didn't even stumble on the *s*. Castor wondered how many times she'd practiced saying it to herself. "Aren't they perfect? One chomp and I could thkewer a mongrel like you. The only thing more pitiful

70

than a dog is a bird. Especially a bird who can't fly."

Castor looked down at the concrete floor. She was right. She was a ridiculous cat with a lisp, but she was still better than he was. Castor was an omega now, the lowest of the low. He couldn't even manage to get food or water for himself, and he would probably be stuck in this cell for the rest of his life.

Hearing a faint clanging, he and Enza both fell silent. Castor recognized the jingling keys and the squeak of sneakers, and he peered eagerly through the glass door. The man was coming back. Castor remembered his guilty expression. Maybe he had decided to set him free!

But the footfalls were the wrong rhythm, and the smell was strange and clean, and the human who arrived in front of them was a short woman with stringy hair and a hard little line for a mouth.

"Slop!" she announced brightly.

Castor cocked his head at her, and across the hall, Enza glowered. Neither had the slightest idea what "slop" meant.

Then, abruptly, Castor heard a loud, grinding sound. He froze, the hackles on his back rising defensively. It sounded like a Crusher Slusher was right in his room!

He shut his eyes tight, convinced he was about to become squashed doggy. But then he heard snorting.

"You thoulda theen your fayth!" Enza scoffed at him. "It's justh a door, you big baby."

When he turned, Castor saw she was right. One of the square doors in the back of his room, the second from the left, was wide-open.

At first, Castor was ecstatic. The one thing in the world he'd wanted was a way out of his prison, and now here was an easy escape, just waiting for him!

But when the grinding sound started up again and a door in Enza's own cell opened, Castor saw the shadow pass across her face—the unease beneath her teasing—and he saw his hope for what it was: naïve. The door was open because the humans wanted it open, and wherever it led was where the humans wanted them to go—nowhere good.

"Slop!" the guard repeated, huffing with impatience, and Castor decided that maybe he wasn't quite so curious about what that word meant anymore. Maybe, he decided, this cold, barren cell suited him just fine.

As usual, though, he didn't get to decide.

The guard took a small gold object out of her pocket. She put it to her lips, puffed out her cheeks, and blew.

"Make it stop!" he howled, pawing at his ears. Though it only lasted a second, the sound was so sharp, so piercing that it sounded like the end of the world.

After the musical torture, he looked over at Enza for sympathy, only to find that her cell was empty. The giant tiger-bear was gone.

"Slop!" the guard said again.

"No," Castor whimpered. She held up the whistle and started to bring it to her lips once more. "I'm going!" he barked, and bounded across his cell in two quick steps.

He stood at the dark void of the open door and, trembling, Castor tucked his new, tender wings close and stepped across the threshold.

12

From inside the dark, musty tunnel, Castor could already hear the commotion. He tried not to panic—the tunnel was so narrow that there was no way to go but forward—but even though he steeled himself to face whatever might lie ahead, when Castor emerged into the light, he was still shocked at what he saw.

The two creatures before him made Enza's bear body seem like a mini's. One was almost as tall as the ceiling, with legs that were thicker than the trees in Castor's dreams. It was hairless, with gray skin stretched like a human's and stuffed too tight, and instead of a nose, it had eight long, waving arms. This must be the elephant, but its trunk was now different.

Castor recognized the other beast from its thick-plated armor—it was Rainner, the lizard from the cages that first day—but he'd doubled in size, and with a new spike of a horn jutting out of his face, he wasn't someone you'd want to make angry. It looked like the other guy had done exactly that.

"FIGHHHHT!" Enza roared beside Castor, as Rainner charged the gray giant. Her feline eyes were dilated with excitement.

"What's going on?" Castor barked in alarm. The hair on his back stood up and he assumed a defensive stance—who knew if he'd be next?

"S-s-samken wanted s-s-some breakfast," a familiar voice answered. "S-s-so did Rainner."

Deja, the snake Castor had met before, slithered past him. All he could do was stare—just as shocking as the other animals' transformations was the fact that Deja hadn't changed. From her pale, diamond-shaped head all the way to the black rattle at the end of her tail, she looked the same as she had before.

Castor didn't have time to ask her how she'd managed

to escape the serum, though. The ground beneath his feet shook as the animal Deja had called Samken crashed around the room. Castor had to leap out of the way just before he was crushed.

"Castor!" someone called to him. He spotted Jazlyn's long, white ears under the food trough. It was the only shelter he could see in the room, and Castor ran to join her.

Though Jazlyn now had a sleek, black cat's body and claws to match, she was as frightened as she'd been before, and Castor could feel her trembling next to him.

"We're safe under here," Castor said, though he wasn't totally convinced of that himself.

"I'm not worried about us," she answered. "I'm worried about Samken!"

Castor looked at the hulking giant across the room. "He looks like he can take care of himself."

Jazlyn shook her head. "He'd never want to hurt anyone. He's way too sensitive."

Castor saw that the gray mammoth was on his knees now, cowering as the horned lizard loomed over him. He remembered what Rainner had said before: *And others are destined to fall.*

"Please," Samken blubbered. "I swear I didn't mean to offend you. I was just hungry." He looked longingly at the food trough, and Rainner slashed at the air with his horn. "Let's be rational about this!" Samken squeaked, snapping his eyes back to his attacker. "You can eat first, and then I'll eat." He fluttered his huge ears hopefully.

But Rainner wasn't swayed. "Kings don't share," he snapped, and lunged for Samken's big belly.

Samken jutted his head forward, his tentacles waving in defense. He managed to wrap them around his attacker's horn and keep from getting skewered, but Rainner grunted and pushed, and the spike inched ever closer to Samken.

Castor's muscles tensed—he should do something! But what good was he against these giants?

"ENOUGH!" a voice boomed, and then there were more horns flying as someone butted his head into Rainner's scaly side, sending him sprawling away from Samken.

Everyone looked toward the new animal. He looked like a horse with stripes, but he had a different animal's face, and two curved and pointed horns stuck out sideways from his forehead, a dark tuft of hair sprouting between them. His nostrils flared as he glowered at Rainner and Samken, sprawled on the floor.

"Do you know who I am?" Rainner sputtered furiously as he got to his feet.

Though the weird-looking horse hadn't hesitated to break up the fight, now he looked wary and exhausted. Castor noticed that all of his ribs were visible beneath the stripes.

The horned lizard didn't wait for an answer. "I am Rainner, a dragon from the island of Komodo, where my family has ruled for centuries. I am the nephew of the Hellion, a fearsome fighter in the Dome. And I am your *king*!"

"Hilarious," the horned horse said dryly. "Well, Your Highness, my name is Moss. Some king you are to get kidnapped and dragged here just like your uncle."

Rainner lowered his horn as if to charge again, but Moss's striped leg shot out behind him, and when his hoof slammed against the wall, the sound was so sharp and sudden that everyone froze.

"I'm sorry to tell you that even kings have to play by the Whistlers' rules," Moss continued as if nothing had happened. "Since I'm the only one here who's been through any of this before, if you want to survive longer than your uncle did, maybe you want to get a hold of your little temper and pay attention? There are only three rules, so even someone with a brain as small as yours should be able to remember them."

Rainner huffed angrily, but he didn't move.

"Great," Moss said, and started to walk around the room, his tail swishing as he sized up the new animals. "Well, since you made it to the slop room, I guess you've all already figured out the first rule: when a door opens, you walk through it. Second rule: when a match begins, you fight. And third rule: when you're not in the Dome, you play nice."

"And if we don't?" Rainner grunted.

Moss's face was grave. "Let's just say there are far worse things than a whistle. Understand?"

"I don't," Castor spoke up. He scooted out from under the trough, climbed to his feet, and shook out his wings. "What's a Whistler?"

"Uh, the people with the whistles. The humans!" Moss said impatiently. "Scientists, guards, vets. The worst are the handlers—you'll meet them soon enough. A word of warning: don't let them think you're weak."

Castor still didn't understand. Not at all.

"But why are they keeping us in this place? What is the Dome? And what's a match?"

The striped bull sighed. "You don't even know why you're here?" Moss walked past Castor toward the far end of the room, and the rest of the animals followed. "We're here to compete in front of adoring fans," he explained, nodding at the back wall.

With all the commotion, no one had noticed the floor-to-ceiling posters. Now, they gawked up at the glossy paper and the bright images.

"It's us," Jazlyn said breathlessly, hopping over to a poster that showed her mid-race, with her panther legs fully extended and her rabbit ears whipping back. "They're all pictures of us."

"Look how big and tough I look!" Samken trumpeted. He used one gray tentacle to point. The picture's perspective was from the ground looking up, so the octo-elephant seemed to tower even taller than usual.

Everyone looked bigger, fiercer, and more impressive on the posters, though. Deja's was an extreme close-up shot, but you couldn't see the diamond pattern on her head or her pale reptilian eyes; her unhinged jaw and two long fangs took up all the space.

Moss's showed a younger, more defiant version of himself, with his striped legs spread wide, straighter horns poised to strike, and clouds of steam puffing out of his nostrils.

"I look like a real hero, don't I?" Moss asked, but his tone was bitter. He looked at Castor with red-rimmed eyes and asked gruffly, "Don't you feel like a hero?"

Castor gazed up at his own illustration. His chest

was puffed out proudly, and strong, spectacular wings reached high above his head. Light shined on his face as he looked off into the distance, chin raised. He felt proud for a moment—maybe he didn't have to be an omega after all—until he saw the writing.

The text introduced him as THE UNDERDOG, which was depressing, but that wasn't what worried Castor most. At the very top of the poster was a banner, and in fancy, slanty font, it read:

THE UNNATURALS

A memory came to Castor suddenly—a flash of the day he was taken. He saw Runt, blinking up at the neon advertisement in wonder.

"We're Unnaturals?" Castor whispered. "The game is . . . real?"

"Real gruesome entertainment," Moss confirmed.

"Where'th Laringo?" Enza asked eagerly. "When do we meet the Invinthible?"

In a sort of daze, Castor walked to the end of the row of posters, where the saber-toothed grizzly was standing. There it was: the white cat's head, the strange scorpion tail—the same image that he'd seen on the building that day with Runt, with the intense, 3D eyes that seemed to track you.

"He doesn't train with us. You don't need to worry about Laringo," Moss said. The bull was trying to sound confident, but Castor caught the defeat in his voice when he added, "At least not yet."

"I'm not worried," Enza purred. "He's the reathon I came here. All I had to do was thlash at a little girl during visiting hours, and I got a ticket to meet the Invinthible."

"You tried to scratch a child?" Samken was appalled.

Enza flashed her toothy grin.

Moss stared at her. "You . . . came here . . . on purpose?"

"Better than staying in Lion's Head Zoo."

This was too much for Moss. He crossed the room and walked in a slow, deliberate circle around Enza, studying her from every angle as if he were utterly baffled by her existence.

"So let me get this straight," he said, stopping in front of her. "You got yourself shipped out of a nice, cushy spot at the zoo so you could make friends with Laringo?" Moss started to snicker.

"What? Just because he's a thelebrity doesn't mean we can't be friends." Enza puffed out her chest. "I mean, we have a lot in common. We both started at a zoo. We both started as tigerth. . . ."

Moss laughed harder, snorting through his nostrils, but to Castor, the laughter sounded strange—it sounded dark.

At first, Enza looked uncomfortable, then annoyed. When Moss started stamping his hooves like he just couldn't stand how funny it was, she got angry.

"You're scared of him, aren't you?" Enza's eyes smoldered and her tail switched. "I heard you didn't even fight in the last match because you were thuch a coward. You're afraid of the Invinthible." The saber-toothed grizzly reared up on her hind legs, which made her almost ten feet tall. She loomed over Moss threateningly. "Are you afraid of me?"

Moss finally stopped laughing, but he wasn't looking at Enza. Castor followed the bull's gaze back up to the poster of the scorpion-tiger. It said THE INVINCIBLE, but in his mind's eye, Castor could picture other text. He saw the sentences scrolling across the advertisement that day in the Lion's Head alley. He could see the words as he'd read them to Runt—two words, in particular, flickering in a capital shout: MURDEROUS MUTANTS.

"Do you know what happened in the final match of

the last season?" Moss asked quietly.

"The Invinthible won," Enza replied.

"Yes, by killing all the other Unnaturals. All of those on Team Scratch and even his own team, Team Klaw. Sometimes it's just common sense to be afraid," Moss said solemnly. "In here, fear is what keeps you alive."

13

MARCUS GOT OFF THE ELEVATOR AT SKYPARK SIX, skateboard in hand. S-Six was a former rooftop farm that had become defunct after the crops died out, and it was the perfect place to practice his kick flips and frontside pop shove-its. It was also pretty much the only place outside the apartment that Marcus was allowed to go—deemed safe because it was as far from ground level as you could get—and even then, his mom would only let him go early in the morning, before the sun got dangerous. That meant Marcus was usually stuck skating alone, like he did everything else.

Not today.

From the entrance, Marcus could see a group of older guys making passes in the dried-up fountain–turned half-pipe, or grinding the edges of the raised garden beds. He rolled his board back and forth under his foot, itching to join them.

"Hey, check it—it's the recluse," one dude said, pointing his way. His grin revealed a chipped front tooth, and he was old enough to have what passed for a scraggly beard.

Marcus was caught off guard by the remark—he didn't expect anyone to know who he was—and he stopped rolling the wheels, feeling a flush crawl up his neck.

"You gonna try something, Bubble Boy?" another called out. "Or just creep all day?"

Marcus was now sweating inside all the padding his mom made him wear, and most of the guys had stopped skating to smirk at him. They didn't want to hang; they thought he was a little baby.

If he could nail a hardflip, they'd respect him—he doubted any of them could do that. Marcus wasn't sure he could, either, but he couldn't just walk away. Not now.

He ripped off the stupid protective gear and started up the stairs with his board.

When Marcus reached the top step and lined up his board, the first guy shouted, "Mean tricks are for big kids, little man."

That got a few chuckles, but Marcus ignored them. This was as much his park as theirs.

Pop the tail, kick flip, then jump, he rehearsed the trick in his head. *Easy.*

He inhaled deeply, getting his courage. Then, feeling the board beneath his feet, Marcus took two hard pushes and kicked off. As the wheels rolled over the edge, he stomped on the back of the deck, then kicked out his front foot to spin the board.

Jump! he thought.

But he was already getting serious air. *Keep it fluid, quick,* and he knew he could land it.

"Marcus! HEY!" someone yelled.

Marcus jerked midair and lost his balance. His skateboard careened away, but he couldn't get his feet back under him because of the steps. Not that there was time—there wasn't even time to put his hands out before he smashed into the concrete.

Then the world went fuzzy.

"Marcus!" Someone was shaking him. "Oh, man,

Marcus, I'm so sorry." Pete was crouched over him, practically cooing with concern as he assessed the injuries.

"I'm fine, Pete," Marcus grunted. Pete was twenty years old and lived in his own apartment, but sometimes Pete would meet Marcus at the skate park on his days off to hang out. Though Marcus wasn't expecting him today.

Marcus sat up, trying to shrug his older brother off him, but a stab of bright pain in his shoulder made him cry out.

"Don't move it," Pete said, pursing his lips. "Something might be broken."

As his brother helped him up, Marcus winced. Beyond the shoulder, his hands and knees were scraped up pretty bad, too. With everyone watching him, he felt like an amateur, but then one of the older guys yelled, "Duuude!" in this voice of pure awe, and some of the others started to hoot and clap.

Marcus nodded at them shyly, and he couldn't help grinning as he followed Pete out of the park, cradling his arm. It must've been a pretty sick trick before he bailed for them to cheer like that, so maybe it was worth it.

But by the time he was settled beside Pete in his aircar, the glory had faded as Marcus realized what the injury meant: his mother was going to flip. He'd gotten roughed up skating before, of course, but those were little cuts he could hide with long sleeves. A broken arm?

"Mom will never let me skate again," he said dejectedly, slumping into the seat.

"Sure she will." Pete hit a button that locked them onto a cable track and then typed in their parents' address at the Eris Escape Tower, floor 247.

"Do you know how long it took me to convince her to let me come to the Skypark the first time?" Marcus asked as they started to glide down the cables. "She wanted me to wear a gas mask, even though the park's enclosed in glass, and then she finally agreed only if I wore zinc sunscreen and an insane amount of padding."

"Maybe you should've been wearing the padding just now, eh?" Pete countered, cocking an eyebrow. When Marcus rolled his eyes, he sighed. "Look, give Mom a break, okay? She's just a little protective is all."

"Understatement of the century!"

It's not like Marcus didn't get why she worried. After their dad died from radiation exposure in the Greenplains, they were all pretty freaked. She wanted to keep her boys close. But there was close, and then there was claustrophobic.

"At least you have your own place," Marcus told Pete.

"Yeah, right next door." Pete rolled his eyes. It was

the only way their mother could cope with the prospect of him moving out.

"But you get to leave the high towers for work every day. When Mom sees my arm, any tiny bit of freedom I had is gone. It's going to be simulated reality and filtered air and sky living for the rest of the summer."

Pete chewed his lip, obviously feeling guilty. Then he pressed something, and the aircar came to a sudden stop. It swung a little on the cable as Pete started typing new coordinates into the navigation system.

"Where are we going?" Marcus asked.

"I'm taking you to the NuFormz facility," Pete answered. "There's a care center there where we can patch you up."

Marcus's heart skipped a beat. NuFormz was on the island where Pete worked with the Unnaturals—the only things Marcus loved more than skateboarding. Bruce was a geneticist there and had helped get Pete a job as a tech when he was first trying to woo their mother. But the island had always, always been off-limits to Marcus. As was pretty much anything outside the high towers.

"Are you serious?" he asked Pete.

"I can fix you up myself, and this way you can have one last hurrah before you're on lockdown. Just don't tell Bruce, okay? I don't really feel like getting fired."

"Like I'd ever tell Bruce anything," Marcus said, offended at the suggestion.

"Come on, he's not that bad," his brother insisted. For some reason, Pete felt like he had to defend their stepdad, even though Marcus could see the way Pete's lip twitched every time Bruce called him "Peter" in that condescending voice of his.

"Not that bad?" Marcus repeated. "Bruce is the enemy of fun," Marcus said.

Pete and Marcus's dad had been fun. He'd been hilarious and goofy and up for any adventure. He was an explorer who took risks other people were afraid to because he thought he could save the world. Bruce was his total opposite, a boring, anal-retentive lab geek.

"He even smells weird," Marcus added. "I still don't get what Mom sees in him."

"Formaldehyde," Pete muttered. "That's what he smells like. But speaking of Mom." Pete wagged a finger. "She'd better not find out I took you to ground level without a gas mask."

"We're not even going outside," Marcus said. "Isn't there an aircar port right in the building?" Pete raised an eyebrow in response, waiting. "My lips are sealed," Marcus promised.

Pete nodded and the aircar jerked to a start again. It

shifted onto a different cable track, this time toward the river, and they zipped down hundreds of stories in seconds. Marcus tapped the deck of his skateboard against the door of the aircar excitedly. It was cool enough to be descending below the fiftieth floor, but to be going to the place where they trained the Unnaturals was unreal.

"You are seriously the best brother ever!" Marcus beamed at Pete. "Major props." He reached over for a fist bump and then grimaced at the ache in his shoulder.

"Careful," Pete said, but he was grinning. And when he ruffled Marcus's shaggy blond hair—a gesture that never got any less annoying, no matter how often he did it—Marcus didn't even pull away.

They were gliding above the river now, with Reformer's Island just ahead. On one end of it, something gold glittered in the sun, and Marcus recognized the rounded roof of the Unnaturals stadium. As he imagined all the newly designed mutants getting ready to fight inside of it, Marcus could hardly remember to breathe.

This was going to be the best day of his entire life.

14

Despite his hopes, Marcus didn't get to go inside the Dome stadium. Instead, they entered the compound through a squat, gray, windowless building on the opposite side of the island, where they took a painfully slow elevator underground, went through a zillion checkpoints, and walked down a maze of hallways that, even though they had the most perfectly waxed floors Marcus had ever seen, Pete forbade him from skateboarding.

It didn't matter, though. Marcus was willing to crawl if it meant he could see the monsters.

First, Pete insisted on dealing with his arm. Marcus expected Pete's lab to be like a factory, full of all sorts of cool tools and wires and stuff for fixing the Unnaturals, but the care center turned out to be a tiny room with a gurney and an antiseptic smell that reminded Marcus of when his dad was in the hospital. It turned his stomach and made his heart feel weird and tight, and he would've walked right back out if it weren't for the promise of mutants.

Instead, Marcus obediently sat on the gurney and let Pete torture him with all sorts of stinging swabs on his scrapes and totally unnecessary gauze wrapped too tight around his knees. Marcus got excited when he saw an X-ray machine—that would've been cool at least—but after making him move his arm into all these wavy, modern dance–type moves that hurt so bad he gasped, Pete said he could tell it wasn't broken.

"It's just a nasty sprain," he said. "You got lucky."

Marcus still had to wear a sling that his mom would notice, and he didn't even get a tough-looking cast out of it.

He turned to Pete, eyebrows raised high with hope, and finally, finally his brother asked, "You ready to see them now, or what?" Marcus leapt off the gurney so fast it collapsed.

"Let's go!" he shouted, and raced into the hallway.

ᴓ

Marcus forgot about the pain in his shoulder as soon as they entered the Pit. He wasn't sure what to expect. Charging stations? Autotransistors? Warp receptors to enable the virtual fight simulation? This looked more like a gymnasium. Hearing the snorts and screeches and stampeding feet, he got goose bumps. He couldn't believe he was really here!

The Pit was at least four times the size of the Skypark, with a twenty-foot high chain-link fence running around the perimeter, and a parrot perched on top. Having spent his life in the Sky Towers, the bird was the first animal Marcus had ever seen. It had brilliant blue and yellow feathers, and eyes that watched him intelligently.

"Don't stare too long at Perry," Pete said under his breath. "Bruce has got that evil-eyed bird trained to report my every move."

Marcus nodded. That wasn't too hard. As beautiful as Perry was, he was the least interesting creature in the room.

Pete wouldn't let him go inside the fence, but Marcus could see plenty from where he stood. The Swift, an animal with a black panther's body and white rabbit's ears, was running loops around the steep-banked track that ran along the gym's perimeter, and every time she streaked past, Marcus's hair whipped around his face. In the center of the gym, other new monsters were training on machines and working with handlers. Marcus watched as a woman tossed basketballs to a giant bear, and it popped one after another with a set of curved teeth so big they almost looked like tusks.

"That's *Miracinonyx ursidae*," Pete rattled off the scientific name automatically. "Saber-toothed grizzly bear."

Marcus nodded. The Fearless. He'd started reading about the new teams the moment the stats were posted to the network feed. The creature turned her head as if she'd heard, fixing them with her golden stare. A long, striped tail swished behind her.

"And there's the Underdog," Marcus said, recognizing the black-and-tan German shepherd–bald eagle mix. He was in the corner, stretching out his wings, and the images on the simulink definitely hadn't done them justice—the span had to be at least nine feet! "Totally incredible."

"Is it really that much better than what you see when you warp?" Pete asked.

"Oh, no, they're exactly the same. . . ." Marcus raised his eyebrows with mock seriousness. "Except for, you know, warp nausea, static interference, and low-res-supposedly-4D visual, versus actually being able to feel the ground shuddering as they run, or watch them move without a fraction-of-a-second time delay, or smell the sweat in the room."

"Mmm, mmm, the sweet stench of animal BO." Pete closed his eyes and sniffed the air.

But Marcus was serious. He peered through the holes of the chain-link fence, watching in awe as the grizzly crushed another basketball. "It's weird that they smell at all—the lab team really went all out. I just can't believe how real they seem."

Pete cocked his head. "Uh, they are real."

"Not, like, real real." Marcus waved his hand. "They're androids. Programmed. Their cells are grown in little Petri dishes in a lab by Bruce and his guys. I mean, don't get me wrong, I think they're awesome! But they're pretty much automopooches, right?"

Pete crossed his arms and peered at him strangely. "Did Bruce tell you that?"

"Yeah. Forever ago, when he and Mom first started dating. Made me swear not to tell anyone that they were really virtual models, but I don't get why it's some big secret. I mean, they're still pretty rad. Why are you look-ing at me like that?"

Marcus's older brother was one of the most mellow people he knew, but right then, Pete's cheeks were flushed a blotchy red and his eyebrows were knotted together.

"So, all along you thought . . ." Pete ran a hand through his hair, searching for words. "Marcus, it's not like that."

"Not like what?" he asked uneasily.

"Some cells are farmed, yes, especially when they need to graft extra skin or build protein for horns. But the mutants aren't just designed from scratch." Pete stepped closer, and Marcus saw the pain in his brother's magnified eyes. "They start off as regular animals, Marcus. And the shot of spliced DNA they receive comes from the bodies of other regular animals—there are donor animals above the housing block."

Marcus chewed his lip and shifted his feet. "What do you mean, 'regular—'"

"I mean *real*. Alive." Pete's voice was quiet but firm, and this time, there wasn't any room for misinterpretation.

Alive?

Marcus fell back against the fence—he felt like he'd been socked in the stomach. He thought of all the blood he'd seen spilled over the years. He thought of how he'd cheered.

Marcus couldn't bear to meet Pete's gaze, so he

peered through the fence at the Unnaturals again, his good hand gripping the chain links so hard his knuckles were white. He recognized the Mighty from last season, and remembered how cheated he'd felt that the zebra-bull didn't fight in the Mash-up, since he was Team Scratch's best shot against the Invincible.

Remembering what had happened to the other animals in that final match, Marcus now saw the misery on the Mighty's face. He saw the fear in the whites of the mutant rabbit's eyes, and the grizzly's anger.

Real animals. Real pain, he thought, aware of the dull throbbing ache in his own arm. He thought of the words *donor animals* and remembered something Pete had said earlier—that the weird smell that hung around their stepdad was formaldehyde. Marcus hunched over his knees, worried he was going to be sick.

"That's why you don't like to watch the matches," Marcus said to the dirt, knowing it was true. Marcus had tried to get Pete to warp in with him a dozen times, but Pete always had an excuse for why he couldn't make it.

"I'm sorry, Marcus." Pete rubbed his back gently. "I thought you knew."

Maybe he had known, somewhere deep down. Maybe the lie was just too convenient. A part of him wanted to go on believing Bruce, even now, to keep enjoying the show, willfully oblivious. But that wasn't who he was.

When the nausea passed, Marcus straightened back up. "How can you stand it?" he asked his brother, unable to keep the accusation out of his voice. "How can you work here, knowing what it is?"

Now it was Pete's turn to look away. He took off his glasses and rubbed his eyes, and Marcus could tell it was something he'd struggled with for a long time.

"I guess I just know someone needs to help them when they're hurt." He shrugged in defeat. "I'd rather it be me they can count on."

Shouts from across the training gym made the two brothers turn.

"Fly! Fly!" a skinny man with a pinched face was yelling. He'd secured weights at the base of the Underdog's wings, and strong, stretchy bands connected the dog's hind feet to a post. The eagle-dog couldn't seem to get even a foot off the ground before he was pulled back down again, his belly skidding along the floor as the bands snapped back. Even from here, Marcus could hear the whimpers.

"Stop it!" he yelled through the fence.

The man didn't hear him over his own high-pitched

shouts, but the parrot did. It turned toward Marcus and cocked its head, clicking its beak together a few times.

"Come on," Pete said, watching the bird anxiously. "We should probably go."

Marcus couldn't believe what he was hearing. He turned to his brother with narrowed eyes. "What happened to helping the animals when they're hurt?"

"Marcus, they're training. They do this every day." He started to guide Marcus away toward the exit, but Marcus shrugged him off.

Instead, he leapt at the chain-link fence. He managed to scramble up it one-handed, still cradling his hurt arm to his chest.

"Marcus!" Pete said in alarm. "You can't go in there! Those are wild animals!"

But they weren't wild, Marcus knew. They were prisoners.

Years of crashing and burning skate tricks had made Marcus fearless and, as Pete fumbled with his keys to get the gate open, he was already hiking his leg over the top bar.

"Alert!" Perry the parrot shrieked next to him, flapping its wings. "Alert, alert!"

"FLY!" the man taunted below.

Marcus dropped to the ground and watched as the

eagle-dog took a few trotting steps, sprang hard from his haunches . . . and was yanked backward like a rock in a slingshot as the bands pulled taught. He yipped once, then sank into a heap on the floor.

Marcus ran toward the injured animal, but before he could reach him, another man stepped in his path and grabbed Marcus by the arm. Though this guy was older, with thinning hair and a gut, he had an imposing frame, and his grip meant business.

"What is a kid doing in my gym?" the big dude growled, looking over Marcus's head toward Pete, who had finally made it through the gate. "Did you forget that this is a restricted area?"

"Sorry, Horace," Pete said, shuffling Marcus behind him. "He's my, um, intern. Can you give us a minute with the Underdog?" he asked, practically groveling. The guy must be a manager or something. "I need to check how his wings are doing so we know he's ready to fight."

The man named Horace frowned and spit right at Pete's feet, but when Pete started pulling medical supplies out of the pouch at his waist, the boss relented. "Give 'em five minutes, Slim," he called to the younger trainer. "Then back to work."

"Fine," Slim answered with a tight-lipped grin. Marcus didn't return the smile.

Horace walked away with a huff and Slim slunk off toward an exit, tugging a pack of cigarettes out of his back pocket. Marcus watched them go with disgust.

Finally, he knelt down next to the animal, still lying with his legs tangled underneath him and his wings splayed out to the side. There were feathers everywhere on the ground, and there was a burnt smell from where they'd dragged on the treadmill.

"You're okay, buddy. It's okay." Marcus reached a hand out, but the eagle-dog flinched away from him.

Carefully, Pete removed the harness, and as he rubbed ointment on the scabs where the new wings had broken the skin, Marcus stroked the animal's soft ears, trying to soothe him. He could feel the eagle-dog quivering all over.

Or maybe it was Marcus who was shaking. He couldn't tell. Everything was so real he felt numb.

15

After the boy left, Castor knew his short moment of relief was over. Castor's handler nudged him with a steel-toed boot.

"Again," he said with a smile.

Slim was a slight man with bulgy eyes and a grin constantly plastered on his face, but the smile didn't mean he was happy—Castor had learned that fast.

Castor scrambled to his feet now and got back into position.

"Fly!" Slim shouted, and Castor tried, really he did, but the bands yanked him back once more, and this time, Slim brought the whistle to his wormlike lips.

The sound split through everything. Castor had thought the guard's whistle was bad that first day when she'd signaled it was time for slop, but that was nothing but a quick toot to get him moving. Slim's whistle went on and on, a high, sharp scream that had Castor on the ground, curled into a ball, shaking.

"Enough!" a voice roared suddenly.

The whistle stopped.

"Horace. You're back." Slim let out a high, nervous laugh. "I, um, didn't see you standing here."

Horace was hard to miss. The Pit's supervisor was shaped like Enza—a solid, square mass of man, with arms coated in fur. Every time he came around, Slim's eyes bugged out even more, and he got all twitchy and nervous, like a rat.

Castor didn't blame him. While there was a cruelty in Slim that crackled with his every movement, Horace was completely detached from Castor's pain—it was like he didn't see him as an animal at all—and that was more terrifying than anything.

"You're messing up training for my whole gym with that thing," Horace growled, and snatched the whistle out of Slim's hand.

Looking around, Castor saw the other animals on the floor, too, wincing from the noise. Now he felt even worse.

"The scouts said this one was tough. Special." Horace frowned down at Castor, who was feeling anything but tough. Then he looked back up at Slim, his thick eyebrows knitting together like two caterpillars. "And I told you the mayor wanted a win for Scratch this season, after all the rioting fans at the Mash-up. I ain't about to disappoint her, not with promotions coming up. Do you want to disappoint me?" Though Horace's voice was soft, you couldn't miss the threat in it.

"No, sir," Slim mumbled, staring at the ground. Now it was he who looked like an omega, all deflated and cowering.

"Then what's the problem?"

"The worthless mutt won't do what I say," Slim whined, and Castor could sense the restraint it took his handler not to kick him again.

"He doesn't respect you." Horace huffed. "You need to make him understand that you're his master. That he does what you say, no matter what." Horace tugged on Castor's harness, coaxing him back to standing, and Castor couldn't help but flinch.

What does "no matter what" mean?

Horace was rummaging around in a cabinet now, and he brought back something that looked like a human arm. He held it out to Slim.

"Put this on."

Slim looked at the object uneasily, but he did as he was told and slid the rubber guard over his own hand.

"Hold out your arm," Horace commanded, and Slim tentatively reached his covered arm toward Castor. "Now watch." Horace cracked his knuckles, leaned over Castor, and said very calmly into his ear, "Attack."

Horace looked Castor right in the eyes, something every dog knew was a direct threat.

"What are you waiting for?" Slim screeched, and the sensitive hairs inside Castor's ears quivered. He thrust his arm forward more forcefully. "He said move!"

Horace held up a hand to silence Slim, which made the smaller man sulk.

"Attack," Horace repeated calmly.

When Castor hesitated once more, Horace lunged. In one smooth motion, he flipped Castor onto his back in an alpha roll, pinning Castor's body on top of his new wings uncomfortably. Castor was shaking all over, and it took everything he had not to howl in despair. Even Alpha had never used the alpha roll because it was so degrading.

Don't let the handlers think you're weak, Moss had warned, and now Castor understood why. Castor felt as cornered as he had felt back on the docks before he was taken here. He was afraid. He missed home. He missed his pack and his brother. He missed feeling normal. Lying in that prone, vulnerable position, something inside of him snapped.

Castor bucked upward, throwing Horace off him. His paws slammed into Slim's chest, and his teeth sank deep into the man's arm. As Castor's mouth filled with the metallic tang of fresh blood, he realized he'd bitten the arm without the rubber glove.

"My arm!" Slim wailed, clutching it to his chest. He stumbled backward and fell on his behind, his feet kicking up sand as he scrambled to get far away from Castor.

"Good dog," Horace said quietly.

Castor looked around the Pit; all of the other animals had stopped their training and had turned to stare at him.

Castor felt a cold unease in the pit of his stomach.

16

MEALTIMES WERE USUALLY NOISY, SOCIAL OCCASIONS where the animals could leave the misery of training behind. It was a time to unwind. And the only time Castor could get water since he still couldn't reach the water bowl in his cell. But when Castor reported to slop that afternoon, there were no boisterous howls, no chatty nickering, no joyful whinnies to greet him.

"That was pretty scary, what you did in the Pit," Samken finally said. He looked up at Castor from under thick lashes, a quiver in his voice.

"I had no choice," Castor explained. After hours of being ground into the floor by Slim's boot, the insistent whistle driving Castor crazy, the unthinkable humiliation of Horace's alpha roll, what else could he have done? "They just kept pushing me harder and harder."

"Most of us don't want to fight each other. But you have to be careful. That's exactly how they trained the Invincible," Moss said quietly.

Castor felt the fur along his spine rise. Moss was staring past the group to the poster of the white tiger head and the arching scorpion stinger, and Castor waited for the veteran Unnatural to say more.

Before he could, Enza cut in with a loud snort. "Castor is nothing like Laringo," she protested indignantly. "Are you all really afraid of a mangy street dog? He doesn't look anything like his poster." She glanced toward the back of the room. "What a joke! I've never even seen him hold up those floppy wings."

In her own illustration, Enza's eyes looked crossed, her fur looked matted, and sitting on the ground like that, with her belly roll hanging to the floor, the grizzly was more flabby than ferocious. You couldn't even see her tiger's tail.

Castor knew Enza was cutting him down now to feel

better about herself, but he was relieved that she'd broken the tension. And looking at his poster made Castor remember something else.

"She's right," he said, trotting over to it. "Even the Whistlers think I'm pathetic, or they wouldn't have called me the Underdog!"

The animals were looking around in confusion, but Deja's glass-like eyes studied him with interest and understanding. "The s-s-shepherd dog can s-s-spell?"

Castor had forgotten that being able to read was anything special, but now everyone was crowding around him, forgetting their trepidation as they asked about their own new identities.

Samken was the most excited about his stage name. He lumbered over to his poster and tried hard to mimic the fierce expression of the illustration. "Could I be the Enforcer?" he asked with a grimace that just made him look constipated. "How about now?" He looked up at the picture and blew out his cheeks. "Hey . . . what's that other writing?" Samken reached a tentacle toward the ceiling.

At first, Castor thought he meant the Unnaturals banner, but then the elephant said, "Right there," and slapped the upper-left corner of the poster. When he pulled the tentacle free with a wet, sucking sound, it left a slimy streak over a paw-print sigil that Castor hadn't noticed before.

Castor squinted. Inside the sigil on Samken's poster, he could just barely make out the tiny red letters. "Team Klaw," he read, and that sent everyone into a frenzy.

"What team am I on?" demanded Rainner, nudging Castor with his horn.

"You're also Team Klaw." Castor tried not to flinch as he answered the armored lizard.

Deja had snaked up Samken's treelike legs to get a better look. Her head waved out in front of his face like an extra tentacle, reaching toward her own red sigil. "It looks like I am, too."

Castor nodded. "So is Laringo. And it says I'm on Team Scratch." He walked along the wall, using his nose to point out the paw prints with the yellow text. "With Enza, Jazlyn, and Moss."

Jazlyn flashed Castor a quick smile. But not everyone was excited. Samken, for one, looked crestfallen.

"But we're best friends!" He reached a tentacle toward Jazlyn's panther tail, giving it a tug. "We have to be on the same team!"

"You're on the winning team," Rainner said. "And we're going to crush the competition!"

He shouldered against Samken playfully—as if the octo-elephant were an old buddy and not someone Rainner had recently attacked over breakfast—but Samken flinched away from him. He rubbed the soft skin of his side where Rainner's armor had scraped against it.

Rainner flashed a reptilian smirk. "Like I said before, some animals were born to conquer." He nodded up at the image of himself, mid-charge. "And others . . ." He smiled at Jazlyn and Castor, his mouth full of pointy little teeth stained with red saliva, and Castor remembered the rest: *And others are destined to fall.*

"The teams don't matter, anyway," Moss said. The other animals turned to look at the striped bull, who was still standing at the trough by himself.

"OF COURTHH THEY MATTER!" Enza, who'd been strangely silent, roared suddenly, and spit flew in all directions.

Those first few days in the prison, Castor had listened as Enza practiced her *S*'s long into the nights. He knew how hard she'd worked to conquer the speech impediment from her saber teeth, so hearing her lisp again now, Castor knew she must be pretty upset.

"I'm not thupposed to be with a bunch of thithies." Enza swiped a thick paw at her own poster, slashing through Team Scratch's yellow sigil. Now that she had everyone's attention, she licked her lips and concentrated hard on the words. "I'm supposed to be with the Invincible."

"You want so badly to be with your hero." Moss studied Enza for a long moment, his jaw slowly working the cud. "Do you even know why Laringo isn't in here with us?"

"He's superior and deserves to be pampered," Enza fired back.

But the other animals were watching Moss intently, waiting for an answer. They'd all been wondering, but no one had dared to ask.

The veteran stepped out from behind the trough so that he could address all of them. "The handlers trained Laringo so well, pushed him so hard, brainwashed him so completely, that now he doesn't just fight on command—fighting is who he is. He's kept apart from us because he'd slash into you at the slop. Claw you through the cells. Sting you in your sleep."

"What about the rules?" Jazlyn asked. "You said—"

But Moss was shaking his gnarled horns. "For Laringo, the rules don't matter. He became what they said he was—Invincible. Unstoppable. And fans come to watch, hoping that someone will beat him. The handlers will drive us into the ground if it makes us want to fight one another. They want someone to put up a fight against Laringo. Everyone loves underdogs."

He looked at Castor and then walked back toward the trough, his tail swishing restlessly.

17

You smell the squirrel before you see him. You smell his brothers, too, urging you on your hunt. You follow their nutty scent through rustling grasses and over ground packed with pine needles. You hear the drumming of their little hearts, the catch in their breath. They scramble up tree trunks and dart through the leaves, but you are closing in.

You come into a clearing and see squirrels all

around you, perched in the branches. Soon you will feast.

But strangely, they are not cowering from your slavering jaws.

They are staring. This is a stadium built of trees, and the squirrels are the audience. They start to snicker, a hundred squirrel voices tittering in unison, and your blood runs cold.

Then you feel it. There's something on your back.

Crawling.

You crane your neck behind you, but no matter which way you look, it's just out of your view. It's creeping all over you, and the squirrels laugh and laugh and laugh.

❧

"Get it off me! Get it off!" Castor howled in panic. He was already on his feet and chasing his tail in circles, tripping over his talons and slamming into the stack of metal weights as he tried to get a look at whatever terrible thing had a hold of him.

But there was nothing there. He was still training in the Pit. After dinner at the slop, Slim had made Castor do another two hours on the treadmill at a grueling pace—probably as revenge for Castor injuring his arm.

Castor must've fallen asleep there after the "extra" training. There was no sign of the handlers and, looking around, he saw that the other animals had all gone back to their cells.

Castor's muscles ached. He might as well catch a bit more sleep before the Whistlers came to get him. Castor collapsed onto the treadmill mat and shut his eyes, waiting for his dreams to carry him back to the Greenplains and far away from here. . . .

Then Castor heard snickering, and his eyes snapped back open.

The squirrels, he thought groggily, but it wasn't a squirrel's voice that spoke to him.

"I heard they brought in another dog."

It sounded . . . canine.

"Hello?" he asked. He peered between the rows of exercise machines, but there was no movement among their metallic arms.

"I heard he took on an entire pack in Lion's Head."

The voice was closer now, and it seemed to be coming from above. Castor tilted his head back and squinted against the fluorescent light . . . and almost jumped out of his skin when he saw the starlike shadow dropping down.

It was hanging directly over him!

Castor tried to scramble out of the way, but his

overworked muscles screamed with each movement.

At the first touch on his back, Castor's body went rigid, and when the eight hairy feet traveled over him, his own fur stood on end. It was just like in the dream—worse than in the dream—and Castor shook his body violently, trying to get it, whatever it was, off him. Finally, the creature scuttled onto the floor, where he could get a good look at it.

The Unnatural standing before Castor was truly hideous. It was part arachnid, that was clear, but not like the tiny spiders whose webs Castor had sometimes seen shimmering between buildings back home. This thing was bigger, hairier, creepier.

Its legs were each as long as Castor's tail, and were made up of four fat segments that started rusty brown near the tips and darkened to a deep blue-black near the bulbous body. When Castor saw the size of the red fangs wiggling between the two front legs, a violent shiver ran through him.

"What are you?" he asked.

"I am Pookie!" the high voice squealed happily, and it sounded so harmless that Castor forced himself to drag his eyes up from those menacing fangs to look at the animal's face. Perched over the spider legs was a tiny head that featured a small, delicately pointed snout, two eyes like brown marbles, and a pair of comically large triangular ears.

"You're a mini!" Castor exclaimed in surprise.

An old mini, which was rare. The fur on the canine face looked like it had once been black, but it was heavily speckled with the white whiskers of age. The hairs that sprouted above the animal's eyes, fanned out of his ears, and dangled under his chin were all white, too, and, instead of the silky texture Castor usually saw on minis, they were long and wiry. He was probably the oldest mini Castor had ever seen.

"I'd prefer that you not use that slur," the mini—the creature—scolded. "You may call me 'Pookie the Poisonous, Unnatural First-class Canis Atrax, Undefeated Chihuahua Warrior of the Streets, the Whistlers, and the Arena.' Or you can just call me Pookie." Pookie's small muzzle stretched into a grin, and Castor saw that he only had a few of his pointy little teeth left. Not that it mattered, though, with those scary fangs. "And who are you?"

"I'm . . ." Castor's talons flexed against the sand. "They're calling me the Underdog. But I'm not even a dog anymore," he said, lifting and shrugging his awkward wings pointedly.

"No," Pookie agreed. "What you are is a heap on the floor."

Castor had felt too tired to get up before, and now he just felt dejected. He sprawled out even flatter on his belly.

"I guess so. Just a jumble of parts that don't work. A mutant. A monster. A freak." He winced, thinking of Perry the parrot.

"Never mind *what* you are right now. Let's start with *who* you are, shall we? What is your name, pup?"

"The Under—"

Pookie held up a slender leg in protest. "Your real name."

"Castor."

"Is that all?" Pookie prompted, bouncing a little to show his encouragement.

"Fine," Castor sighed. With his chin still resting on his paws, he mumbled, "I'm 'Castor German Shepherd, Descendent of the Mexican Wolf and Third Dog of the Trash Mountain Pack on the Southside of Lion's Head.'"

"Good!" Pookie lifted Castor's chin with one of his sticky feet, and when he spoke, his voice was surprisingly firm. "Remember who you are, pup. Always remember that first, and you will take away their power. They will try to take many things from you while you are here, but they cannot take that."

"They already did!" Castor whined. "I don't have any

of that anymore. I'll never see my pack again." He'd been trying to put his old life out of his mind, and the thought of his pack mates, of Runt and Bill Bull and even Alpha, made his eyes glisten and his heart ache.

Pookie was less sentimental.

"Perhaps you will." The Chihuahua-spider cocked his head matter-of-factly. "Or perhaps not. But perhaps you must find your new pack in here." He gestured one of his many legs around the empty Pit.

"New pack?" Castor was indignant. The thought of replacing his family was more than he could bear. "A pack is something you're born into, not something you join."

Pookie didn't argue with Castor. He just stood there patiently, smiling his little smile, swaying on his legs, and waited. It was maddening.

"Besides, I don't think the animals in here really trust me yet, anyway," Castor added with a groan.

"Show them, then. Show them you deserve their trust. Show them who you are, deep down inside." Pookie reached out a long, hairy leg to tap the white patch in the middle of Castor's chest. "Show them how your spirit soars."

Pookie flexed his eight legs and sprang high into the air over Castor's head.

Castor was about to say that it was too late, that his spirit had already been broken, when he remembered something: Moss had said that he and Laringo were the only veterans. Castor knew there were unchanged animals in other levels of the prison, but he hadn't heard about any other mutants.

"Hey," Castor called behind him. "Where did you come from, anyway?"

When Pookie didn't answer him, Castor turned around to see where the many-legged mutant had landed. He wasn't on the track or on top of the treadmill. And in the rafters, there wasn't a trace of web.

Pookie had disappeared as quickly as he'd come.

PART TWO

UNDERDOGS

"All New Season of Unnatural Mutants!"

*"Fan Fatigue: Low Sales Show Scratch
Skepticism on Opening Day"*

"Can Newbies Challenge Reigning Champ?"

18

Castor hadn't let himself imagine his first fight. He didn't even know how to fly yet, let alone fight! He'd refused to think about monsters or Domes or Laringo or the strange quiver in Moss's voice when he'd talked about the matches.

Instead, Castor had focused on getting through each minute of each long day. He'd focused on training hard and sleeping deep. He'd focused on the repetitive exercises in the Pit, the careful chewing of the gruel, and the grinding sound of the tunnel doors in his cell that marked the passing of time between them: Slop, Pit, Slop, Pit, door two, door three, hour after hour, day after day.

And it had all become so routine that when Castor heard the rumbling of cement one night, his ears didn't even twitch. It didn't even occur to him that he'd just eaten an hour ago or that it was too late in the day for training.

Not until he turned around.

At the back of his cell, for the first time, the door on the far left—door number one—was wide-open. It was the door Moss had warned them about: the door to the Dome.

Castor was afraid all over—in his heart and his gut, in his muscles, and deep in his bones. He felt the fear, cold as ice, pumping through his veins. But at the NuFormz facility, obedience came before fear. When a door opened, you walked through it. So Castor made himself move toward the ominous black hole in the wall before the guards did.

When he stepped, trembling, out of the other side, Castor was surprised to enter a tiny room instead of a huge arena, and to recognize the familiar faces of his handlers instead of an anonymous crowd. He wasn't ever happy to see his handlers, but today the sight of Slim and Horace filled Castor with relief.

Then Slim snarled, "Where have you been, mutt?" and kicked him, and the feeling passed.

The holding area was blazingly hot, and Slim had lit one of his fire sticks, so the air was choked with smoke. Castor's eyes watered and his nose burned and he was panting like crazy from the heat, but he was happy to stay in here forever if it meant he could put off the fight a little longer.

Slim clipped a leash on Castor and yanked him over beside him, but otherwise, the handlers didn't pay him much attention. Horace sat on a chair with his thick hands clasped together, and Slim leaned with one foot against the door, and both men stared intently at a little box that hung on the wall.

From down on the floor, Castor craned his neck to get a better look, and he couldn't believe what he saw. Inside the box, he could see the other captives so clearly—from the tiny stripes on Enza's tail to the diamond design on Deja's skin—that at first he thought the Whistlers had shrunk them. Castor barked in alarm.

"Quiet!" Slim blew a quick, shrill toot on his whistle, and Horace turned to glower at him for the interruption.

His ears still ringing, Castor looked back at the box. He saw the light glinting on the screen now, and he realized it must be glass or a virtual image, like he'd seen on the buildings in Lion's Head. Still, the match was as real as anything.

Deja slithered around the perimeter of a large, circular clearing—looking for a way out, Castor guessed—while Enza stalked the center, tracking the snake's progress.

"What are they doing?" Slim peered at the screen. "Why aren't they fighting?"

The audience seemed to be getting impatient, too. Castor could see them standing up in their seats and waving their arms, and though the volume on the box was turned off, he could hear the boos through the walls and feel the vibration of the sound. Castor's own nerves returned—he hadn't realized the arena was so terrifyingly close.

"Maybe they need a little nudge," Horace said. He wheeled his chair backward and hit a big red button with his palm. "That should do it."

In the little box, the screen seemed to blur, until Castor understood that it was the animals that were blurring—Enza and Deja were both shivering strangely. Castor wasn't sure what was happening, but he knew it couldn't be good. Despite his fear of Horace, he leapt to his feet and barked at the big man.

Enough! he growled. *Stop hurting them!*

"Easy, Underdog," Slim snickered. "You'll get your turn soon enough."

But Horace was already lifting his hand, and when he released the red button, the two animals seemed to understand what they had to do, and immediately took off toward each other.

The match had finally started.

Enza crouched like a practiced huntress, her body quivering and ready to spring toward her prey. But though the grizzly-tiger's pose was distinctively feline, she seemed to sense the awkwardness of her huge, lumbering body, and instead of lunging, she danced away from the snake's zigzagging advances.

"I thought we were gonna see those sharp sabers flashing!" Slim pouted. "And why is the Cunning still on the ground?"

"It's like this every season," Horace explained. "Their old instincts are still kicking in."

A bear would have stood up to its full height and used its weight to swoop down and stamp at the snake with its giant front paws. A saber-tooth might have swiped at the reptile with its knifelike incisors. But Enza crept low to the ground like a cat, failing to make use of her new body.

Still 100 percent snake, Deja seemed much more comfortable in her own skin. She slashed a side-winding pattern across the floor of the arena toward the grizzly-tiger, forcing Enza back into a corner.

Suddenly, Deja shot forward, snapping her fangs as Enza defensively batted the snake away.

Both animals regrouped, circling each other, hissing.

Castor glanced up to see the wet underarm circles staining Horace's shirt and heard the anxious rhythm as the man tapped his foot. He tensed instinctively—an unhappy handler in a tight space could get nasty.

On the screen, Deja's tail rattled and her head struck forward; this time Enza was done dodging. They clashed together in the center, their bodies locked in a vicious embrace. As the Unnaturals rolled heavily across the sandy ground, the people in the audience were on their feet cheering.

The two Unnaturals were so tangled up it was hard to tell who was who, but Deja's scaly body looked stretched tight, and Castor thought that Enza's furry brown arms looked awfully limp. . . .

"Come on, you're supposed to be fearless!" Horace shouted at the screen suddenly, his face reddening. "At least use your claws!"

The handler punched the red button again, but this

time he held it down too long. Castor could see the whites of Enza's eyes, and the length of Deja's body bunched into one tightly clenched muscle. It took a long time for their bodies to stop shivering, and when they did, the stillness was even scarier.

Castor started to pant and whine in distress, pawing at the box.

Why did Deja look all crumpled like that? And why was Enza's tongue lolling out on the dirty sand? Why weren't they moving?

They didn't stir even when a pair of Whistlers came out to drag them off the field, and the announcer called the match in Deja's favor. Horace swore and slammed his fist onto the table.

"You really wanted that natty teddy bear to win, huh, Horace?" Slim joked. It wasn't often that the young handler had the chance to hold something over his boss.

Horace glared at Slim as if he had the intelligence of an earthworm. "The shocks help them break their original instincts. And like I told you, the mayor wants Team Scratch to perform better this season."

"Why is the mayor such a big Team Scratch fan all of a sudden?" Slim gave Horace a sideway glace.

"You think Mayor Eris really cares about the team, you nitwit? No, she wants ratings. If no one thinks the

Invincible can be beaten, then why watch the matches? It needs to at least seem like Team Scratch *could* win for once. Which means if the eagle-dog doesn't perform like he did in the street, certain bookies are going to be very unhappy with the odds they were given." Horace got very close and spoke into Slim's ear. "You ever been on Vince Romano's bad side before?"

Slim's chin dimpled uncertainly, and when he looked down at Castor, he actually frowned. "He's ready."

"He'd better be."

Castor tore his eyes from the screen and looked up at the men. He didn't know if he could ever win. But he did know he was the furthest thing from ready.

He started to back his rear end under the table, but there was nowhere to go. Horace tugged the leash attached to his collar, and when Castor didn't move fast enough, he snapped the metal chain against the floor. The sound crackled almost as bright as the whistle. It was enough to make Castor walk nicely out of the room and into the elevator, but when Slim pulled the sack over his head, he totally lost it.

The rough fabric clung against his fur, and Castor could hardly breathe. He shook his head, trying to get it off, and when that failed, he howled for mercy. But Horace and Slim didn't have mercy to give. Instead, they taunted him, jostling him roughly between them, until finally the elevator shuddered to a stop.

It didn't matter if he still didn't know how to fly, or if he was scared, or if Enza and Deja were hurt, or worse. Tonight, ready or not, Castor, the Unnatural Underdog, would make his debut in the Dome.

19

Castor heard the muffled voice of his handler say, "Show 'em what you got, mutt," and in the next instant, the bag was ripped from his head, he felt the shove of a boot against his hindquarters, and he stumbled forward out of the elevator, sprawling face-first onto the ground.

If Castor had thought watching Enza and Deja's match had prepared him for what to expect in the Dome, he was wrong. It was an assault on his senses and, at first, he was too overwhelmed to move.

The stadium spotlights were blinding, the shouts of the crowd deafening. The dust from the Dome's floor had risen in a cloud when Castor fell, and it coated the back of his throat and tickled his nostrils. It did nothing to dull the heavy scent that hung in the air, though. The Dome smelled of the stress of animals and the sourness of men.

When his vision had adjusted to the light, Castor saw a vast, circular arena. The walls around him rose twenty feet high, and above them, humans peered down from their seats. He had never imagined so many humans could exist. They had faces of every color, and every age. Some cheered and some leered and some shouted at him, but they all wanted one thing: to see him fight.

Alone on the field and exposed from every side, Castor had never felt so very small.

He wasn't alone for long, though. Far across the Dome, two red doors slid open, and another figure stepped into the arena.

If Castor had found Rainner intimidating at the slop, that was just a preview. Under the bright lights of the stadium, the Komodo-rhino looked every bit the king of dragons he claimed to be. His armored body seemed as big as a Crusher Slusher. His scales were an impenetrable armor. He held his head high in the air, as if his horn was spearing the sky.

The humans got even louder then, the noise so big it hurt Castor's ears and made him dizzy, and they were no longer faces, no longer men, just an unending wall of enemies barking as one.

"We've got so many more WOWZA new magical monsters for you this evening!" a voice, louder than all the other voices, announced.

Castor didn't know where it was coming from—it echoed all around the arena. Then he saw her, near the gold ceiling high above them: a human woman who walked on air.

"Get ready to meet your favorite new mutants," she said, and her body flickered like the ads in Lion's Head. "Because the Underdog . . . is here . . . to take on . . . the Vicious!"

The lights dimmed, and the crowd quieted, and Castor learned that the only thing worse than the humans' noise was their silence. Now he could hear his own heart, racing as fast as a bird's. Then, the bell.

The match had started.

Rainner didn't hesitate like Enza and Deja had. In the low light, his dark silhouette was already moving across the field, and Castor finally understood why sometimes Jazlyn and Runt completely froze up.

Not only could Castor not move, he couldn't even breathe, and now there was a stronger, more pungent smell in the air that he recognized: the smell of his own fear.

Do something! he thought.

But what could he do? He could hardly run without tripping on his talons. He couldn't even get off the ground when he tried to fly. The walls towered up around him, and there was a sea of people beyond them. Horace had told him to show them what he had, but Castor had nothing.

Castor was just a scrappy street dog, and this was no alley fight. He didn't stand a chance.

Thick legs thundered toward him. A lizard tail swung side to side. Black ruthless eyes had him in their sights.

Castor backed up against the locked elevator door. He adopted a defensive posture, but his tail was between his legs, and as Rainner advanced closer, and closer still, Castor's mind was too jumbled to form any sort of plan.

All he could think about was how Rainner's jaw had unhinged while he ate at slop. Castor remembered the red saliva and the pointy teeth, and he knew Rainner was going to swallow him up whole.

Remember your training, he thought, trying to shake

the image from his mind. *Remember Moss's tips. Remember how you fought in the alley.* . . .

What Castor thought of instead was the advice that strange spider-dog, Pookie, had given him: *Remember who you are, and you take away their power.*

Who was he? He was Castor German Shepherd. He was Third Dog of the Trash Mountain Pack. He was a brother to Runt, a pack mate to Alpha, a friend to Jazlyn.

He was not a monster, no matter what the advertisements claimed. And he wouldn't let them turn him into one, like they had Laringo. The old Castor never would've turned tail and run, but he also wouldn't have fought for anyone but his pack.

Horace had said he didn't have a choice, but that was a lie. He was trapped now, like he'd been on the dock with Runt. And just like then, he had a choice about how to go out. He could choose what the Whistlers wanted, yes. Or he could choose dignity. He could choose honor. As the outline of Rainner's rhinoceros horn dipped down, taking aim, Castor chose to lift his head up proud, face his opponent head-on . . .

And sit down in the middle of the field.

To Castor's surprise, the lizard-rhino slowed and then stopped just short of him, sending a thick cloud of dust flying up all around.

"What are you doing?" Rainner demanded. He was already breathing hard from the run.

"I won't fight you, Rainner."

"We're in the middle of a match." Rainner's face muscles were all twitchy with rage. "We're supposed to fight. You're supposed to fight back! Do you expect me to just attack you while you sit there?"

"If that's who you are," Castor said, and his eyes flicked toward that awful horn, "then, yes."

"If I'm going to win—and I'm going to win—I'm going to win fair. You're just going to be a coward and give up?"

"No," Castor said, and sat up straighter. "I'm not going to be a coward. Not anymore."

That's when the collar at his neck started to buzz.

"Do you hear that soun—" he asked, and then a charge went through him, making his teeth chatter and his muscles spasm.

So that's what the red button was for.

Rainner's reptilian eyes glinted with amusement. "Ready to fight me now, eagle-dog?"

Castor shook his head and held firm, and a second wave of electricity brought him to the ground. Another jolt locked his jaw shut. Soon he was seizing and foaming at the mouth. It felt like his whole body was on fire.

But despite the pain, despite the collar at his neck and the high walls around him, for the first time since he'd been captured, Castor felt free.

20

"WELL, THAT WAS A SURPRISING TURN OF EVENTS!"
Matchmaker Joni Juniper appeared as a 3D hologram
floating above the Unnaturals arena as they hauled the
eagle-dog away. Joni was known for charming the audience with her chipper voice and insider knowledge, but
even she seemed shocked by the Underdog's refusal to
fight. "Never fear—there's more Unnatural fun on the
way. Sit tight if you're bozo for bulls or elated by ellies,
because coming right up, the Mighty and the Enforcer

will share their first dance under the big lights!"

Leesa sat perched high atop the post that held one of those big lights, hidden from view—if anyone happened to look directly toward her, they were sufficiently blinded not to notice a gangly-legged girl in combat boots enjoying a free show.

Well, not enjoying, exactly. Enduring.

Unlike the rest of the cheering crowd, Leesa was not, in fact, "bozo for bulls" or "elated by ellies." Nor had she been "gunning for grizzlies" or "razzed by rattlers" in the first fight of the night.

Even though Leesa had seen almost every Unnaturals match in the last four years, she wasn't a fan. She'd only ever come for Pookie.

Leesa heard the echo of feet hitting the ladder rungs in the hollow chamber below her. Her best friend, Antonio Romano, no doubt. They always watched the matches together from his brother's special seats.

Vince knew everyone—he and his gang pretty much ruled the Drain—and he'd once convinced an electrician who'd been doing work on the stadium's industrial lights to dig a hole under one of the hollow light posts so they could run a ladder up it from an underground tunnel. Ta-da: free tickets to the best spot in the Dome!

Antonio's thick, dark hair emerged from the hole,

and Leesa noticed he'd slicked it back so it barely curled. Just like his older brother, Vince's.

"Leesa." He paused on the ladder when he saw her. "I wasn't sure if you'd be here."

Leesa shrugged. "It's opening night. I'm always here, aren't I?"

Though after what had happened that night at the final match, she wasn't sure she'd ever come to the Dome again, either. In the end, the possibility of seeing Pookie, no matter how slim, brought her back once more. As much as she hated watching the animals suffer, Leesa wanted to believe that if she was there, if she was watching, Pookie would know. That she could protect him, somehow—especially now that she knew no one else would.

"Always." Antonio grinned and passed her a plate of food. "That's why I got you these."

Pineapple chili zingers, drenched in oil. It smelled like heaven.

"You didn't have to do that," Leesa said. She knew how expensive fruit was, especially with the food rationing in the Drain. Still, she wasn't going to turn down pineapple zingers. That would be crazy! She took the plate so he could climb up, and scooted over to make room for him.

"No biggie." Antonio flashed his snaggle-toothed grin and tugged playfully on her braid. "I know they're your favorite."

She popped a zinger in her mouth. "Thanks," she said, savoring the burst of juice.

"Don't thank him." Vince climbed up off the ladder after Antonio. "This meal comes to you compliments of . . ." He pulled a stack of cash codes from his pocket and spread them like a hand of cards. "Mrs. Strout."

Vince was six years older than Antonio—almost nineteen—but they could've been twins if Antonio put some weight on his tall bones and grew a goatee. Leesa knew he would if he could; Antonio worshipped his brother. Sometimes that meant doing a lot of pretty dumb things to try to impress him.

"We swiped them from a couple of tourists on our way in," Antonio was boasting now, more for Vince's sake than hers. "The high risers were all too busy cooing over the catatonic bear."

"Consider it the rich tax for invading our territory!" Vince said, toasting the crowd.

Antonio got in plenty of trouble, but she'd never known him to steal. Leesa shifted uncomfortably and set down her plate of food.

"Aw, come on, Lees," Antonio teased, seeing her

expression. "You think anyone is going to give us what we want? We have to take it."

That sounded like another Vince-ism to Leesa, but she kept her mouth shut.

"So what did we miss?" Vince asked, peering over her shoulder.

Leesa opened her program and leaned away from him—his cologne always made her gag. "You missed '*Canis accipitridae*, a stunning mix of courageous canine pedigree and majestic eagle aerodynamics,' battling against '*Varanus rhinocerotidae*, a combination of sturdy rhinoceros armor and a Komodo dragon's knack for eating enemies alive.'" She rolled her eyes at the dramatic description. "The eagle-dog lost."

"The Underdog was a dud? Let me see that." Vince squinted at the stats page, his mood darkening in an instant. "My guy on the inside told me that mutt was a real killer."

"He refused to fight," Leesa reported with a shrug. "He sat down in the middle of the arena."

The first match was the most important because it gave the bookies an idea of how the teams would shake out. Inside knowledge was precious, and Vince sold it at a premium to high-stakes gamblers who adjusted their odds with every scratch, settled debts on the fortune of a hunch, staked lives on the strength of the newest science—guys like her dad. And if that knowledge was wrong, well, Vince had earned his reputation for a reason.

"Horace is under my thumb after this." He crumpled the program in his fist. "That goon is going to owe me so big."

Leesa looked down at the current match. The Mighty hadn't taken long to herd the Enforcer into a corner and quickly pinned the octo-elephant's neck with a razor-sharp horn. Checkmate. The Mighty was the only veteran left from Pookie's season aside from Laringo, and it showed. The timid, gentle, gray giant didn't stand a chance. Handlers quickly swarmed the ring to break the beasts apart—no one truly wanted major injuries this early in the season.

Leesa thought about the Underdog. The things she'd told Vince were true, but while the crowd had chanted, "Coward!" that wasn't what Leesa saw. She watched that poor creature jerking in pain as they tried to shock him into submission, and even though she knew this couldn't end well, she found herself smiling at the Underdog's determination. It reminded her of Pookie. . . .

We have to take what we want, Antonio had said.

But what if the one thing you wanted in the whole world had disappeared without a trace?

21

THE CELL DOOR OPENED, AND CASTOR BLINKED UP AT THE hulking figure standing in the doorway, cast in shadow by the bright fluorescent lights. It was not yet dawn.

"You think the rules don't apply to you, eagle-dog?" Horace asked. He stepped forward into the cell and cracked his knuckles, then he reached out a meaty hand and grabbed Castor by the scruff of the neck.

Castor's nails curled on the cement floor, searching for purchase to resist.

"Fine," he snarled. "We won't play by the rules." Then, while the rest of the animals still slept, he dragged Castor away down the hall.

Horace hurled Castor into the Pit, where Slim was waiting. He looked red-eyed and twitchy, and Castor guessed his handler was about as happy to be there at this hour as he was.

"This one forgot how to fight," Horace said, chaining Castor's collar to a post. "Maybe you didn't teach him good enough."

"Oh, he'll get a lesson, all right." The thought of payback seemed to improve Slim's mood considerably.

Castor couldn't help but wince instinctively. When he refused to fight Rainner, Castor had just done what he thought was honorable. But the Whistlers had no honor, and pain didn't end in the ring.

Let them be the monsters, Castor thought as he watched Horace prepare the treadmill and the tension bands for his wings. *All you need to be is a mutt.*

And though Castor gritted his teeth for a brutal training session, soon his howls could be heard echoing down every hallway in NuFormz.

22

In the morning, Castor felt like a new dog. Better than that: he felt like himself again.

Not great, exactly. His body ached like one big bruise from the handlers' special attention, and he'd missed slop for a bath so that one blessedly careful Whistler could clean him up. He was hungry and exhausted. Still, when Castor walked back into the Pit to join his teammates, his head was held high.

The Unnaturals were usually strictly monitored

during training, but Horace was sleeping in the office after his late night/early morning with Castor and, without a supervisor, all of the lower-level handlers were pretty lax. Castor and the other animals were left to warm up on their own.

In the training lane next to his, he spotted Enza. Last night, Castor had watched the Whistlers drag her off the field unconscious, but now the grizzly was hurling her body against one of the thick support posts that held up the towering ceiling. She smashed her shoulder into the post again, and Castor felt the ground vibrate beneath his paws. Despite their differences, he was really relieved to see she was all right.

Jazlyn was zooming around the track that ran along the outside of the fence. At first, Castor worried she'd still be wary of him, but when Jazlyn saw him watching, she skidded to a stop by his side. Her dark spotted panther coat already had a sheen of sweat on it.

"Castor, you look awful!" Jazlyn's eyes were round with concern. "When you weren't at slop, we all wondered what had happened!"

"I'm fine." Castor pawed the ground, embarrassed that they'd worried about him—and relieved anyone cared.

"Was it the booster shot? I got one, too, for losing."

She held up a paw to show him the cotton swab secured with gauze. "They called it 'incentive' to get better."

"No, I didn't get a shot. Just a beating."

Jazlyn shook her head bitterly. "The Whistlers can be so cruel."

"Only Laringo's perfect," Enza said, lumbering over to join them.

For once, Castor was happy to agree. Laringo could have perfect all to himself.

"Jazlyn must be close, though. You're looking faster than ever on the track," Castor told her. It wasn't just flattery, either. She was finally starting to seem comfortable with her panther DNA, and her long legs worked in mesmerizing rhythm as she ran.

"Aw, thanks, Castor." Jazlyn bowed her head shyly, and one of her long, white ears flopped forward. "Since they printed the Swift on all of those posters, I figured I should try to live up to my nickname, you know?"

"That was slow for a big cat," Enza scoffed, unimpressed. "I hunted mice that were faster than that in the zoo. You gotta go harder if we're going to have a shot at winning."

Castor had to smile. Enza could use some work on peer encouragement, but at least she seemed to be warming up to the idea of being part of Team Scratch.

"I'll push it full speed in the match," Jazlyn promised. She stretched a leg behind her, curling her toes and arching her back to get out the muscle kinks.

For Enza, that wasn't good enough. "You have to be consistent. You have to be just as solid when no one's watching."

"Aye, aye, Captain," Jazlyn said brightly. She gave Castor a look that feigned exasperation, but she was still cheerful as she walked back onto the track.

"Faster out of the gate!" Enza yelled.

Jazlyn nodded and crouched into position. Her body froze, her ears twitched, and the short, blue-black fur along her spine stood up as she focused intensely on the sloped track ahead of her. Then the rabbit-panther shot forward, faster than any machines Castor had seen in Lion's Head—even the Crusher Slusher.

The grizzly rumbled up onto her hind legs to get a better view as Jazlyn rounded the corner. "What kind of turn was that? Do you think Rainner's going to have trouble with a sharp pivot when you face him one day?"

Castor knew from experience that Rainner's low-to-the-ground, turned-out lizard legs made him an ace at the quick strike. Enza had an undeniably sharp, critical eye, and now she was using it on him.

"Speaking of Rainner, what was that little charade in

your match last night? I knew you were pathetic, but I didn't think you were a coward."

"He's not a coward."

They turned to see the old, striped bull leaning against the low wall of his training section, watching them.

"It takes guts to break the rules like that, especially in a match," Moss said gruffly. "It's stupid, mind you, but it takes guts."

Castor hadn't done it to be brave, he'd done it to be true to himself, but the bull's compliment meant a lot regardless; Castor didn't realize how much he valued Moss's approval until now.

"I'm not a fighter," he told Moss earnestly, holding the veteran's gaze. "If the Whistlers thought I was, it's because I defended my brother against a dozen dogs who wanted to hurt him. I would've done the same for anyone in my pack, and I'd do it for any of you."

"Now, don't get arrogant," Moss chided, clacking his teeth together. "You might've saved your brother on the street once, but you can't protect anyone in here."

There was a catch in the bull's voice that made Castor think of those other animals Moss rarely spoke about— his teammates from last season. It scared him, but it was Moss who'd told him that fear was a good thing.

"Well, I can try," Castor said. "After all, you're the closest thing I've got to a family now."

"Some luck you have," Moss wickered, giving Enza the side-eye. The giant grizzly was distracted by a piece of rope hanging from one of the machines, and she looked like an awkward, oversized kitten as she batted at it. "This family couldn't get more dysfunctional."

The humor had returned to the veteran's voice, though, and Castor felt the tension between them settle as quickly as the sand Jazlyn had kicked up around the track. Relief buoyed his spirits for the long day of training that lie ahead.

It was tempting to be the lone wolf, always looking over your shoulder, but the true Castor, the Castor of the streets, needed his pack.

23

I<small>T HAD BEEN THE LONGEST DAY OF TRAINING IN HIS LIFE</small>, and Castor was exhausted. He'd dozed off at the dinner trough, nearly drowning in his gruel, but now he was finally back in his cell for lights-out. Castor settled down on his lumpy excuse for a bed, grateful to give his beaten, bruised body a rest. He could already hear Enza's deep snores rumbling on the other side of the wall, and he shut his eyes, eager to escape to his own dreams.

But just as his breathing started to deepen, he heard

something—a scuttling sound, close. Castor's body went rigid.

There was someone in his cell with him.

Was it Horace and Slim coming for him again? Maybe last night was just the beginning. Maybe he was in for another beating. Maybe the punishment would never end.

"Please," he whimpered into the darkness. "Just leave me alone."

"Did I frighten you, young pup?" an old voice croaked.

Pookie.

Castor looked up and saw the spider-dog clinging to the wall, his tiny face crinkled with amusement. The old mutant scurried down to the floor, still chuckling.

"No." Castor's body relaxed, but adrenaline was still surging through his veins. "Well, maybe a little," he admitted. "The way you just appear out of nowhere, and sneak around and crawl all over everything is just . . . blechhh!" He shuddered.

"Creepy?" Pookie offered, wiggling several of his legs in front of Castor's face suggestively.

"Kind of," Castor admitted.

Pookie didn't seem offended. "It is a natural reaction."

He bobbed his head proudly. "And one that has served me well in this prison."

Speaking of prison . . .

Castor looked around—all the doors were still locked. "How did you get in here, anyway?"

"Pookie has his ways," the mini answered vaguely. "The important thing is not how . . ." He gestured dramatically with one of his furry legs. "But why?"

"Okay . . . ," Castor said. He flattened his ears back and lolled his tongue out in a yawn. "Why are you in my cell in the middle of the night?" All he could think about was sleep.

"I saw what happened in the exercise center."

"With the team?" Castor perked up. "You were right—I just had to show them I could be trusted."

"Excellent, pup. You let your spirit soar." Pookie nodded with a small smile. "But I meant late last night, with the handlers."

Oh.

"You were there?" Castor thought of the humiliation he'd endured, the pain.

The wiry whiskers that sprouted from all over Pookie's face twitched with concern. "Maybe you wish to discuss it?"

Castor groaned and lay down his head. Now that he was finally done with training, he wished to get some sleep, not think about his handlers.

But as proud as he'd felt of his peaceful protest during his first match, that beating was no joke, and Castor was going to have to figure out a plan for next time. He wanted his spirit to soar, but he didn't want to die to make that happen.

"It just seems like no matter what I do, I can't win," he sighed.

Pookie nodded, waiting for him to continue. But Castor's thoughts were restless and, despite the fatigue, his legs were, too. He got up and stretched, and started to walk around the perimeter of the room, venting to the old dog.

"I follow the rules and grovel like an omega, and the Whistlers hurt me. I stand up for what I believe in and break the rules, and the Whistlers hurt me. If I do what they want, I hurt others." He was walking faster now, huffing with agitation. "What else is there?"

"Slow down, young pup." Pookie sprang in front of Castor, cutting off his path. "No matter how many times you zigzag around the cell, you will keep hitting walls. You need to look in another direction for your answer."

Castor peered out the glass door of his cell, but the

cell block was silent, the mutants were asleep, and the guard was slumped in her chair, preoccupied with the virtual screen that hovered in front of her face. He looked back at the Chihuahua blankly. "Where's that?"

Pookie pointed a long, hairy leg straight at the ceiling. "Up," he whispered, his small snout stretching into a grin. "You learn to fly."

"Fly." Castor didn't share the spider-dog's excitement. "Last time you told me I needed to remember I was a dog. Now you want me to be a bird?"

Pookie sighed impatiently. "It is still you inside." He tapped Castor's chest like he'd done in the Pit, but this time, it felt more like a jab. "No matter how you look. That is most important. But this is also you." He picked up a long, gray-and-white feather from the floor, and held it in front of the dim light. "You don't have to lose yourself on the inside to accept yourself on the outside."

Castor snuck a peek at the feather Pookie was admiring. It was half white and half dark gray, and it sloped to a graceful point. It didn't feel like a part of him, but he could admit that it had a pleasing shape.

"And your life will be much easier and happier and perhaps much longer if you make the humans think they're getting what they want."

Castor looked up at Pookie, not sure he'd heard him

161

right. That went against everything he believed in.

"But Horace and Slim want me to be vicious," he protested. The thought still made his belly ache.

"No. Look deeper, pup. This is not about you; it is about pack order. Men have to listen to an alpha just like anyone else. Look, here is your handler, Slime, the omega."

Pookie sprang sideways and landed low on the wall, gripping the cement just a foot or two off the floor. He looked at Castor sideways.

"What he wants is to keep his supervisor, Horror, happy."

He jumped again, and Castor's eyes followed his arc through the air until he landed halfway up the opposite wall.

"And Horror, he wants to make the mad mayor woman happy."

Again, Pookie leapt to the other side of the room, higher still.

"And what the big boss wants, most of all, is to keep the fans happy."

Now, Pookie soared all the way up near the ceiling and landed on the wooden perch that held the water dish.

"And how do we make sure the fans are happy, young pup?"

"Um." Castor was half paying attention. He was thinking about the water he was still unable to reach and licking his parched lips. He only got his fluids from the gloppy gruel at slop these days.

"We give them a *show*!" Pookie announced, and Castor's attention snapped back as the old dog leapt from the bar, somersaulted twice, and shot his spider legs out to the sides, gripping opposite walls with his sticky feet so that he was suspended between the ceiling and the floor. Then he pulled all eight legs in close to his body, free-falling in a tight ball.

"Watch out!" Castor gasped, sure Pookie was about to splat on the cement.

But at the last second, the spider-dog uncurled on a thread, landing gracefully in front of him with hardly a whisper.

"And then we survive." Pookie grinned. "And everybody's happy."

"Wow." Castor blinked at the old acrobat. "That was . . . uh . . . something."

"Thank you." Pookie bowed graciously.

"But what about me?" Castor didn't get how some somersaults were going to help him with the handlers— or in the arena for that matter. "I don't have skills like that. I can't even fly." He strained to lift the foreign, feathered appendages off his back, then let the wings fall back down.

"You will. For now, you fake it for the fans. That's half the battle."

24

CASTOR DIDN'T SEE HOW HE COULD PRETEND TO FLY—
that seemed like a disaster waiting to happen—but
Pookie's advice about faking it for the audience got
the wheels in his brain turning. For instance, what if it
wasn't just the tricks that he was exaggerating? What if it
went beyond that?

What if, rather than pretending to fly, he pretended
to fight?

At slop the next morning, Jazlyn and Samken

worried about having to battle each other in an upcoming match.

"I won't do it," Samken was saying tearfully. "I won't hurt my best friend."

"I'll be fine." Jazlyn reassured the big guy with a few pats on the back, but she sounded nervous herself; Samken could crush her with one blow.

Listening to them, Castor's tiny thought turned into a Big Idea: What if *all* of them decided to fake it?

"Maybe there's a way you don't have to fight," Castor said.

"Yeah, maybe," Enza said with heavy sarcasm. "Maybe we can all just walk out of here."

But Jazlyn blinked up at Castor hopefully. "How?" she asked with a twitch of her nose.

"You act like you're fighting, make it really convincing, but you don't actually fight, and you make sure not to hurt each other."

"Like a game?" Samken asked excitedly. "I love games!"

"Exactly," Castor said, but some of the others were skeptical.

"I don't understand," Rainner said. "Why would you want to just pretend to win?"

"Or lose?" Enza frowned. "Where's the glory in that?"

"You preferred the glory of losing for real?" Deja

asked with a flick of her forked tongue. "You didn't seem so fearless-s-s to me."

Enza was still sore that Deja was declared the winner of their matchup. Her massive paws were clenched and Deja's head was swaying tauntingly, but Castor stepped between them.

"It's not about glory," he said. "It's about survival. It's about beating the Whistlers."

That got their attention, and now the rest of the mutants were starting to lean in toward Castor. Even those who looked forward to fights, like Rainner and Enza, would rather beat the Whistlers.

But Moss's brow was deeply furrowed, and his nostrils flared. "I told you, no one wins against the Whistlers," he insisted. "We're just pieces in their little game. Even Laringo. Even you, Castor. You saw what happens when you break the rules."

"I'm not talking about breaking the rules." The Whistlers could just decide to change them, anyway, as Horace had shown the other night. "I'm talking about something bigger. I'm talking about changing how the game is played."

"How do you plan to do that?"

"Give the fans a show," Castor said, thinking of Pookie. He jumped into the air and ran in circles a couple of times to demonstrate. "If we control the crowd, we control the Whistlers."

"I want to decide the routines," Enza demanded.

"Would I get to improvise?" Samken asked, waving his tentacles dramatically.

"Sure." Castor wagged his tail. "We can do whatever we want."

"As long as no one gets hurt," Jazlyn said.

"Why should we trust you?" Deja asked, slithering forward. "Why trus-s-st us-s-s?"

"Because like Moss said, the teams don't matter. Because we're all Unnaturals," Jazlyn answered.

"That's not quite what I said," Moss protested.

Trust was hard in a place like this, Castor knew—especially when that giant picture of scorpion-tailed Laringo still haunted the back wall, reminding Castor that play fighting was only a temporary solution that wouldn't work when they finally had to face the Invincible. But he'd made the leap with his teammates, and he certainly trusted Team Klaw more than he trusted the Whistlers. At least this would help them all survive a little longer. At that thought, he spread his wings above his head and pawed the ground, determined.

"Because if we decide we're really all in this together," Castor said, "then we don't have to be afraid anymore."

25

You wake without a whistle to jar you from sleep or a whip to snap you to attention. Instead, you stir as if from a long nap on a lazy afternoon, stretching your paws out languidly and blinking away the dew.

You are in the place you know but have never been. The place you've missed so much but can never remember. You're in the free place.

The green place.

The green is different this time, though. You don't see the dusky green of moss-speckled tree trunks around you, or the leafy green of a canopy above. No jungly green vines hang nearby, either. All you can see is a flat field of grass stretching in all directions.

The field is a green so bright it makes your eyes water. It smells like the sun. Your fur is warm, the ground is cool, the bed of grass is soft, and your breathing becomes shallow. You think you might like to go back to sleep.

You start to doze again, but your senses snap to attention when a flock of birds startles out of the grass. They are plump birds with white collars and green heads. You see their webbed feet outlined against the clearest sky, and you feel a strange kinship with them, though you don't understand why.

Your claws press into the dry earth, and they are the hard, blunt nails of the German shepherd. When you arch your back to stretch, the thick, buff coat of the Mexican wolf bristles. You are all dog, and the ducks remind you that you should find water and maybe something to eat.

You stand, shaking the dust from your hide.

You can smell the pollen in the air and the earthworms underfoot. A sound rustles through the grass, and your ears stand at attention. It's like a whisper of wind—shhhhhh—but instinctively, you know it is the sound of prey, calling you.

As you start to trot through the field, your tail is a proud flag waving behind you. You are a hunter now. Confident, carefree, canine.

The grass parts up ahead as something slithers through.

Shhhh.

You give chase. Your heart quickens. Saliva drips from your jaws. Your body is a coiled spring, ready to pounce at first sight.

But the grass is growing taller and thicker around you, and the wind whips it into waves. You've lost sight of the path.

The sun beats down. Your tongue feels thick in your mouth. It might be time to give up the hunt.

You pad to a stop, listening for that hissing sound. There is only the wind.

The wind and, faintly, the varied calls of insects. They chirp and buzz, but as you listen, the sound gets louder, growing into a singular, urgent hum. *It starts to sound like a warning, and your adrenaline spikes.*

The grass is over your head now—too high to see which way is out. You push forward with your chest, anyway, but the dense weeds push back. You turn in circles, and burrs snag in your fur.

You wish you had a view from above. You wish you could see what's coming. But all you can see is the green pressing in.

RUNNNNN, the bugs drone.

Then, abruptly, they stop, and your heart almost explodes with the silence. You no longer feel like a hunter; you feel completely exposed. Hunted.

The buzzing starts up again just as suddenly, loud as ever. Only it's not an insect buzz this time, you realize.

It's a rattle.

You crouch down low. Crawl on your belly through the weeds. You wait in silence for a few minutes. Then you hear it.

Closer, closer.

An endless, ominous sssss.

26

A RUSH OF WATER HIT CASTOR FULL IN THE FACE, YANKING him from sleep.

He sputtered, trying to figure out if he was dreaming or drowning or hallucinating. There was no dirt under his taloned feet, only concrete. Wet concrete. Was there a flood?

Castor glanced around him in the dark, but other than his sopping muzzle and a small pool on the floor, everything else looked dry. Then he spotted a red plastic dish lying overturned on the floor—his water dish.

Castor looked up toward the perch at the top of his cell where the dish had sat and, in its place, there was Pookie, hanging gymnastically from the perch by one of his many legs.

Castor shook the sleep from his head and sighed. "Was that really necessary?"

"You were howling and panting in your sleep," the old dog said. "I had to find some way to wake you, and you don't seem to like when I crawl on you."

Castor shivered at the thought of those tiny little hairs tickling him. "Well, thanks, I guess."

Pookie was staring at his pillow, which was now a mess of shredded blue foam. "Bad dream?" he asked.

Even now, Castor could almost feel the hot sun beating down on him, and he was panting as he tried to cool off. His fear lingered, too—he could smell it on himself—but he batted a paw dismissively. "It was nothing."

"Good, then. Are you ready?"

"To . . . go back to sleep?" Castor asked.

"To begin our training!" Pookie squeaked with excitement. He hurried down the wall until he was standing in front of Castor, bobbing giddily.

Castor groaned. The last thing he wanted to do was train in the middle of the night—especially when he wasn't being forced at whistle-point by Horace and Slim—or Horror and Slime, as Pookie called them. But his next match was tomorrow, and Castor knew he needed the extra practice. And Pookie's little flipping routine had been pretty impressive. If a veteran of the arena wanted to offer Castor his help, he'd take it.

"There is just one thing, young pup." The old dog's tone was solemn, and Castor looked up expectantly. "You must make me a promise that you will not speak of me to anyone."

"Sure," Castor answered. If *he* could sneak out of his own cell, he'd be trying to find the nearest exit, but if Pookie would rather creep around, visit other cells, and spend his nights giving advice to newbies, that was his business.

"Excellent." Pookie rubbed his front two legs together.

The spider-dog scurried around the cell, quickly clearing the mat and straw out of the way, and then he directed Castor to stand in the center of the room. Castor stretched his front paws forward and arched his back. He flexed his talons to loosen up his ankle joints. He rolled his shoulder muscles, shook out his wings.

"What you need is focus," Pookie told him. "Let's begin by meditating on a mantra."

"A what-sa?"

Pookie grinned, exposing his pointy canine teeth. "A mantra is a word that motivates you. A word that has power. It's from a practice called Tai Chi."

Castor assumed that was short for *Chihuahua*. He thought for a moment. A word that had power . . . "Like alpha?"

Pookie shook his head. "Something stronger. Something that will give you courage in the arena." He rose higher on his spider legs, as if puffing himself up. "Something that will remind you of who you are and who you need to be."

Brave, Castor thought. "I have it," he told Pookie.

"Good. Now focus on this mantra. Breathe in . . ."

Castor closed his eyes, picturing the word and the warrior that went with it.

"Breathe outttttt."

Castor took a deep, cleansing breath.

"Now look up," Pookie instructed. "And start flapping your wings."

Castor set his sights on the perch above him. *It looks so far away,* he thought, letting out a heavy sigh. Then he started to flap.

"Look at this posture." Pookie clicked his tongue against his incisors in disapproval. "Keep your shoulders even." He popped up and landed lightly on Castor's

back, pushing his muscles down to the proper align-
ment. "Weight back on the feet, eyes forward, toes facing
front. Are you part eagle or part duck?"

"I'm mostly dog, remember?" Castor grumbled. The
shift in his posture felt awkward, and his new wing muscles ached from the effort of opening and closing them.
"And how do you know what I should do? It's not like
you have wings."

"I happen to be a scholar of biology," Pookie answered.

"You can read, too?" Castor asked, surprised.

"No." Pookie shook his head. "But you'd be surprised
what you learn hanging around these halls."

That led to over an hour of Pookie lecturing him on
the details of bird anatomy as he lounged in a newly con-
structed hammock web, and Castor flapped his wings.
And flapped. And flapped.

Pookie might be able to tell him in theory how to
control the small bones in his wings and guide the delicate feathers, but he couldn't unlock the secret of how to
get off the ground. Castor had to learn to do that himself, and right now, that seemed impossible.

"Focus!" Pookie insisted.

"Look, it doesn't even matter if I know how to fly in
the match tomorrow." Castor let his wings flop down in
exasperation. "I'm up against Deja, and she hasn't been

transformed like the rest of us; she's just a snake."

Castor still didn't understand why the Whistlers had a regular, unchanged animal fighting among the Unnaturals. Still, the rattlesnake had managed to hold her own in the arena so far—Castor remembered how she'd beaten Enza in that first match by squeezing the grizzly in a fierce hug.

"Ah, that is easy, then," Pookie said. "You must beat Deja the way a dog beats a snake."

"How's that?" Castor hadn't encountered very many wild snakes in the alleys he'd grown up in.

"On the ground. You can still impress the crowd. Add a leaping flourish here, a dive-and-roll there, but it'll be mostly a running game."

Running, Castor could handle. He might not be totally used to his long talons yet, but he'd had plenty of experience tearing around the streets of Lion's Head.

"What are you waiting for?" Pookie asked from his hammock. He gestured around the perimeter of the cramped room. "Start running!"

By the time Pookie finally called an end to their first lesson, Castor was soaked with sweat and panting loudly. He really wished Pookie hadn't dumped that water.

"We will train every night," Pookie vowed. "Until you are strong, yes?"

The way Castor's muscles were throbbing, "strong" felt about as unattainable as getting to the Greenplains. But looking at Pookie's confident grin and sparkling eyes, Castor found something more precious than strength: he found hope.

The spider-dog tucked in his little chin, flattened his arachnid body against the ground, and slipped right under the door.

So that was how he did it. Castor was starting to understand the advantages of being miniature.

"Pookie?" Castor called after him through the glass. Pookie raised a white, wiry eyebrow. "Thanks."

"Get some sleep, pup," the Chihuahua told him. "After your first match, you already grabbed the attention of the fans. Tomorrow you must win their hearts."

27

BEFORE HIS MATCH WITH DEJA, CASTOR SAT PANTING IN the holding room again, waiting for the other competitors to finish their fight. But this time, watching the little box didn't make him anxious. Seeing his friends' familiar faces on-screen actually helped calm his nerves.

If Samken was intimidated by the crowd, he certainly didn't show it. He was a natural performer, tossing his head around so that his huge ears flopped, and waving to the crowd with his many-tentacled trunk.

Jazlyn was rooted to her spot in the middle of the sandy circle, but Castor knew that was part of the act—the fans knew her as a quivering bunny, after all.

When Samken had the audience where he wanted them, on their feet and shouting his name, he turned toward Jazlyn, lowered his formidable tusks, and charged.

Thundering across the arena, Samken's body looked like an unstoppable boulder, and if Castor hadn't known better, he'd think Jazlyn was about to be crushed.

Just before he barreled into her, Samken blew through his many mutant trunks, sounding what appeared to be a war cry. The cacophonous trumpet made the people in the stands cover their ears, but for Jazlyn, the signal was clear as a bell.

She took off.

With her sleek cat's body, Jazlyn was like a machine built for speed. Her spring-loaded rabbit hind legs provided the power, and her long panther forelegs shot out to gain distance with each stride. If Samken seemed fast before, now he looked like a broken-down tank, sputtering and groaning as he lumbered after her.

Horace jumped to his feet and shook his fists at the box. "That's right, Swifty, make him dizzy, tucker 'im out."

Then Jazlyn abruptly pivoted on sure-footed hind

legs and zipped right toward Samken. She leapt, sailing over his head, but the giant swung his tentacled trunk, snatching her out of the air.

Wow! They were really putting on a show!

. . . At least Castor thought it was a show. He didn't remember this part of the routine.

Castor leaned past Horace to look closer at the screen, searching for some sign of reassurance. But as Samken struggled to his feet, he was still clutching the rabbit-panther tightly, and all Castor could see peeking out of the slimy grip was one of Jazlyn's floppy ears.

He could see Samken, though, and to Castor, it seemed like a switch had been flipped. The usually timid, goofy giant looked crazed, and as he started tossing his head back and forth, shaking Jazlyn in the air, he seemed a hundred times more terrifying than his poster.

He looked like the Enforcer, all right. He looked like a monster.

Does that ugliness lurk in everyone? Castor wondered with a shudder. *Do we all have shades of Laringo simmering just below the surface?*

Castor was starting to lose hope, and when the octo-elephant uncurled his trunks and Jazlyn tumbled limply across the sandy floor, it seemed like his worst fears had come true.

The hushed crowd leaned forward in their seats, watching as Samken reached one of his tentacles toward the still, dark form, his expression uncertain.

That's when Jazlyn exploded upward, spun in the air, and shot her two hind legs forward toward the broad gray face, nailing him right between the eyes.

It looked like a stunning blow, and Samken's eyes rolled as he stumbled right, swooned left, and fell to the ground with a thud, sending up a cloud of dust. It was funny and dramatic and the crowd absolutely loved it.

Samken hadn't turned and Jazlyn hadn't died; they'd both delivered the performance of a lifetime.

28

CASTOR BURST INTO THE ARENA FEELING CONFIDENT AND calm, ready to wow the crowd with his bag of tricks just as his friends had. There was Deja, at the other end, her diamond-shaped head held poised, watching him.

It'll be mostly a running game, Pookie had said, so Castor trotted across the field, eager to see what impromptu choreography they could come up with.

He moved in quickly and agilely, dancing around in front of Deja and snapping dramatically toward her.

"This is going to be fun!" Castor said.

Deja grinned at him with amusement, and Castor only vaguely noticed that her tail was twitching.

"Listen for that shake, shake, shake of the rattle, snake supporters!" the sparkly woman said from above. A drumroll sound effect filled the auditorium, and the audience joined the announcer, shouting: "Wwwwwatch out, baby!"

The serpent's head struck out like lightning, and Castor didn't realize that he recognized the awful rattle from his dream until it was too late. The bite was so fast Castor didn't see it coming, but when Deja's venomous fangs sank into his nose, he sure felt it.

"Why did you do that?" Castor let out a high-pitched howl and shook his head back and forth, pawing at his nose to try to stop the anguish.

Deja's cold eyes bore into him. She didn't seem to understand the question. "Because life is safer when you are the first to strike."

"But it would've been safe if we pretended to fight, like I said. I trusted you!"

"That was s-s-stupid," Deja said simply. She wound herself into a tight coil and flicked her forked tongue, meeting each of Castor's protests with a flash of her fangs. "I wouldn't even trust one of my own kind, let alone a mangy street mutt."

"What about sticking together? What about winning against the Whistlers?"

"I've survived this long by being on my own."

Each time Deja lashed out at him, Castor barked and batted at his attacker. But her jabs were coming a little too close for comfort, and he was afraid of another attack to the face. Castor backed off, stumbling toward the other side of the arena.

As the venom did its work, Castor was starting to feel disoriented. His nose was already swollen so much that it was hard to breathe, and all of his senses were feeling a bit fuzzy. Still, Castor thought he heard the familiar rattle of Deja's tail.

Not that again.

Across the field, the snake was zigzagging toward him, all right, and her erratic movements were impossible to predict. But Castor wouldn't give her the chance to strike a second time.

Though he might be the Underdog, Castor had never been one to roll over and give up, not even for Alpha. Castor rooted his feet into the earth, steadying himself, and took a running start. His legs were strong even as other parts of him started to weaken, and Castor bounded back across the field in a few powerful strides. It looked like he was about to collide with Deja, but instead, Castor pushed hard off the sand, snapped his enormous brown-and-white wings out to the sides, and leapt. Then he flapped like his life depended on it.

Perhaps because it did, for once, amazingly, his feathers did not fail him. His wings were beating open-close, open-close, and he wasn't tumbling back down to the ground.

He was flying!

The announcer's voice perked up with excitement. "A smart, strategic move from the already-wounded Underdog. Folks, this match just got interesting!"

Not that it was pretty. Castor figured out that each time he slid his shoulder muscles down his back, the wings flapped, but that didn't help him much. He had no idea how to control the wings themselves, no clue how to make his feathers lay flat enough to slice the wind, or how to get the angle right to make a sharp turn. He careened in awkward circles, dipping dangerously close to Deja with each uncertain swoop.

Still, a few people might actually be cheering for him now and, despite how nauseated he felt from the venom, Castor's heart swelled with pride.

Maybe the tide was turning?

But below him, Castor watched as two scales snapped

back on the sides of Deja's winding body. They looked almost like gills, but then something silky and bright was unfolding, pushing its way out of the folds, and Castor realized that Deja had transformed and that no one, including him, had noticed. Just like some snakes have retractable fangs, Deja had retractable wings!

And it looked like, unlike Castor, she knew how to use them. He couldn't beat Deja on the ground, *as a dog beats a snake*, but fighting in the air wasn't looking much better. Deja, the creature that Castor had only ever seen slinking on her belly along the floor, was now floating almost as high as the gold ceiling.

This snake was just full of secrets.

Deja's wings looked nothing like Castor's; they were whisper-thin and featherless and reminded Castor of the moths and butterflies he'd seen fluttering around the streetlights of Lion's Head. Her wings glowed with a diamond rainbow pattern that matched her scales.

Deja decided to take them for a test run by swooping down on the crowd and diving toward their seats. At first, the people in the bleachers were leaping out of their seats and throwing up their arms, but once the humans got over the idea of a deadly mutant monster snaking over their feet, they loved her.

As she floated back up, the movement was so subtle

that it looked like Deja was pinned in the middle of the air. She wasn't pinned, though, as much as Castor might've wanted her to be.

"The Cunning might look as pretty as a painting, but this serpent of the air still has her hunter's instincts intact. See that flick of the tongue? That's how snakes smell, and it means she's tracking our furry friend," the announcer narrated, and Castor's stomach dropped.

Castor needed a plan, and fast. He no longer seemed to have the advantage of the sky, so he dipped down and hit the ground running once more—well, limping, but at least he was more comfortable than in the air. When Deja floated toward the ceiling, presumably preparing for another strike, Castor headed for the outer rim of the ring, hoping to buy some time.

"The Underdog isn't frozen this time, Moniacs!" the announcer proclaimed. "The wolfish warrior is on the prowl!"

Castor didn't think he was prowling, exactly. He skulked close to the edge with his wings tucked in tight at his sides, so it would be harder for Deja to get a clear drop on him. He went around and around the field, keeping a wary eye on the snake trailing him from above.

"Get 'im, Cunning!" people were calling. "Squeeze the Underdog till he pops!" The crowd was getting impatient with Castor's circling. They sneered at him as he passed, and some were throwing things. He flinched and pulled his ears back when a cup full of fizzy, brown liquid exploded against the wall behind his head. Pookie said he needed to win the crowd's favor, but they were turning on him!

So was Deja—again.

While he was preoccupied with the humans, she'd somehow gotten behind him. Castor felt a cloud of sand swirling at his feet, but he realized too late that it was the wind from Deja's strike. Her rattle sung its brief warning, but before Castor could even turn, Deja had buried the two points of her fangs in his ankle.

"S-s-sorry." She smiled up at him in her unhinged way.

Howling, Castor limped a few steps, paused, swayed, and then collapsed.

Still, he noticed something as he lay there in the packed stadium, struggling not to lose consciousness: the audience wasn't cheering for his fall this time. Instead, they were hushed. They were waiting for him.

With so much venom working through his veins now, Castor felt like he might lose consciousness at any moment. *Brave, brave brave,* Castor recited the mantra to himself though his feverish haze. *Just get up. Be brave enough to save yourself.*

Deja was coming for him on the ground again. Her bright wings folded back up, she had just a snake's body again, quick and unpredictable. And this time, because of his injured leg, Castor couldn't run.

Deja's head lashed forward to deliver a final, deadly blow, and Castor jumped, snapping his wings open faster this time and tucking his legs up tight. Then, before Deja could even swivel her head, Castor dove back down and, with the talons on his uninjured front paws, snatched Deja right up.

It took all his remaining strength to beat his wings and all his concentration to hold her. She was furious, and her slippery body thrashed in his grip, her tail shaking angrily. But Castor held her just behind the head, his talons tightening around her neck so her jaw was locked shut. Deja could rattle all she wanted, but there was no way she could bite him now.

As Castor hovered in the air over the bleachers clutching the snake, he didn't feel majestic or fearsome. His wings were tired, his body was shuddering with toxic poison, and he felt like he'd lost more in this match than he'd gained.

"Ladies and gentlemen," the floating woman began. Her eyes were misty, her voice full of feeling. "I present to you, the winner of this match." Then the cameras zoomed in on Castor, and he saw his own face projected all around the Dome. "This is no Underdog. I think we can all agree, tonight we've seen the bravest of the brave, the eagle-dog!"

Castor sighed in relief, swooped low enough to drop Deja onto the sand as the handlers rushed in, and blacked out.

29

LEESA WAS SITTING AT A DESK IN MS. HOILES'S MAKESHIFT classroom, puzzling over some algebra, when her tablet buzzed. It had to be Antonio. No one else would bug her in the middle of the school day.

Meet me at the ladder.

Leesa stared at the text for a minute, curious. Her friend meant the ladder to the Dome, of course, but they'd just been to a match last night—the Underdog battling the Cunning, which had been almost as hard to watch as last season's final Mash-up—and the next Unnaturals' fight wasn't for two more nights. She tapped out a quick response.

Can't. School. Remember?

Antonio's reply came in almost instantly.

Ditch.

Leesa rolled her eyes. Antonio wondered why her mom thought he was a bad influence; maybe it was because he'd been trying to get her to drop out since she'd moved underground four years ago.

Come on, Lees. Better than spending the day with the Grubbs.

Leesa giggled. Her classmates were a runny-nosed brother and sister who whispered about her in nasally voices. Minnie Grubb shot Leesa a nasty look now and hunched over her math work sheet, guarding it like her answers were precious.

Leesa chewed on her stylus, considering. It was tempting. . . .

Ms. Hoiles glanced at her over the rims of her glasses. "Everything all right, Leesa?"

Leesa nodded and set the tablet back on the table next to the copy of *Charlotte's Web*, which she'd finished and meant to return.

Ms. Hoiles picked up the worn paperback and leaned against Leesa's desk. "Did you like this one?" she asked, thumbing through the pages.

"Very much." Leesa beamed. She loved all books—the feel of them, the smell, the escape they offered—but this one made her feel powerful, like she might have something special in her that could change things.

Ms. Hoiles must've seen some of that in Leesa's eyes, because she smiled and said, "Keep it."

"Really?" Leesa squeaked. The antique seemed so rare and fragile, so beautiful, she couldn't believe anyone would want to just give it away. But Ms. Hoiles pushed the cover toward her.

"It isn't often we stumble upon things we really love, is it?" she asked with a smile. "Just take care of it."

"I will!" Leesa promised, nodding rigorously as she hugged the book to her chest. "Thank you!"

Then she put her head down to get back to work, but it was hard to concentrate. She kept thinking about what Ms. Hoiles had said, and she only got through two more math problems before her tablet buzzed again.

Come on. Just an hour. It's special.

Something about the text or the book or the luck of the day made Leesa reconsider this time. She felt guilty for leaving after Ms. Hoiles had been so nice, but she knew she had to go. She looked up at her teacher apologetically.

"I'm really sorry," she said, and gathered her things. "Something at home."

On her way out, Leesa glanced at the text again, at that word—*special*—and started to run.

❧

Antonio was leaning against the door to the ladder as he said he'd be, but instead of climbing up to the stadium like they always did, he beckoned Leesa farther on down the tunnel. It was dark and damp, and Leesa's boots made splashing sounds as she followed him. When they stopped, Antonio pointed up, and Leesa saw a circular hatch.

"What's that?" she asked uneasily.

"You'll see." Antonio grinned, and rapped his knuckles three times on the iron door. He had a charged look to him, the bright eyes and wolfish smile he got when he was excited about something—usually something mischievous.

Leesa heard screws twisting from above, and then the lid started to come loose. Antonio took the circular disk from an unseen hand, and his arm muscles strained with the weight. Once he'd set it on the ground, they were blinking up through a hole into the harsh light of the sun.

Leesa was shocked by the sight of it—it had been a long, long time since she'd been outside, but more than that, she was shocked by the stench.

"Is that sewage?" Leesa wrinkled her nose.

"The river. You'll get used to it in a sec." Antonio heaved himself up out of the hole.

"But we don't have gas masks," she called up to him, her voice echoing in the tunnel. Her mom said everyone wore gas masks now, because of the pollution. "Or sunscreen."

"Still a sky kid at heart, aren't you, princess?" another voice scoffed.

Vince. No matter how many years Leesa had spent in the Drain, Antonio's brother would never let her forget that she wasn't really one of them. He reached a hand down to help Leesa up, but Leesa ignored it, wriggling into the sunlight by herself.

When Leesa stood up, her boots crunched on a beach of gritty sand, and she took a deep breath, blinking in the sunlight. The smell was even worse now, but after spending most of her time underground in the artificial light of the Drain, it was still amazing to be really, truly, outside.

Even if Vince was here to . . . what? Babysit them?

Leesa raised a questioning brow at Antonio, and Antonio glared at Vince, and Vince held up his hands.

"All right, lovebirds, I'll leave you alone," he said with a laugh, which made Leesa feel even weirder. "I have an appointment at NuFormz, anyway."

NuFormz? Leesa's ears perked up at the name.

"We're on the island?"

"Yeah." Antonio gestured over his shoulder. "There's the Dome." Leesa had never seen the Unnaturals stadium from the outside, but she still recognized the iconic round roof. Beyond that, Leesa could see gray, windowless buildings set back from the water.

"Are we going in, too?" Leesa asked, the hope blooming inside her chest. Maybe that's what Antonio meant by "special."

Vince raised an eyebrow, but Antonio was shaking his head. "To the compound? No. But there's something cooler than that, anyway," he insisted, tugging her toward a steep bank. "Come on."

In the fierce heat, Leesa was already starting to sweat as she followed Antonio toward the blue arch of a bridge. It led across the river—but they weren't on the Lion's Head side of the shore, Leesa noticed.

"I didn't know there was a bridge to the Greenplains," she said.

"They closed it to traffic after the radiation accident a few years back," Antonio said, and Leesa peered past him at the construction signs and caution tape. "Now it's all ours."

He used his gangly arms to climb up the supports on the river's edge, but Leesa didn't swing up after him. Instead, she turned back to look at Vince, who had already started up the gravel path that led to the NuFormz compound.

"Wait!" she called down the path suddenly, and Vince turned. "Is there any way you can get us into NuFormz? Please?"

"Lees, no." Antonio had jumped down now, and his high cheekbones flushed red. "That's not why we're here."

But how could it not be? Now that they were so close to the place where her Chihuahua had been taken, how could Antonio expect her to be thinking about anything else besides Pookie?

She shrugged off Antonio and ran to catch up to Vince. "You said that guy owes you a favor, right?" she asked, breathless from the smoggy air.

Vince nodded. "Horace. But I don't owe you a favor, do I, princess?" Vince's expression was hard to read—it hovered somewhere between amusement and offense.

"Leesa . . . ," Antonio warned.

"What?" She glared at him. "He said I have to take what I want, right?" When it came to Pookie, she was sick of waiting and wondering. She looked Vince in the eye and pulled her shoulders back, standing up straighter. "Well, the only thing I want is to see the mutants, so are you going to take me or not?"

Vince's poker face fell apart, and he chuckled. "She's sassy! I see why you dig it, Tony." He elbowed Antonio, who coughed, making a strangled little sound, and Leesa could feel her face flushing red. "All right, Princess Leesa. Ask and you shall receive. Let's go see the mutants."

30

"You're doing so good, buddy."

Castor panted in response as the medic called Pete hunched over him, loosening the electric collar. Pete had already given him an antivenom injection, but Castor's jowls and neck were still so swollen it was hard to breathe.

Castor's nose stung from the chemical-clean smell of the floor and the metallic tang of surgical tools. Somehow, he'd ended up back in the little room where he'd first transformed, and back on the same table.

Trying to ignore the needle Pete held between two blue-gloved fingers, Castor focused on the medic's face—the hairs speckling the angular jaw that were so pale and fine they were only visible when the fluorescent light shined on them; the wire circles perched atop a narrow nose, magnifying eyes that crinkled with concern; the lips pursing in a thin line of concentration.

Pete's face blurred in Castor's vision. It was so hard to stay awake. He felt so weak. . . .

Pain jerked him back to consciousness, though, and Castor yipped.

"What did you do to him?"

Castor recognized the voice of the boy he'd once seen in the Pit—the one who had tried to protect him. From where he lay on the table, though, Castor couldn't see him.

"Quiet, Marcus!" Pete scolded. He had bent over sideways and seemed to be looking under the table. "I told you, if anyone finds out I let you in here again, that's it, I'm fired."

The boy's head popped up from beneath the white sheet that covered the table. The wide blue eyes stared right into Castor's.

"I am being quiet," he grumbled. "But you're not supposed to hurt him more. Look at him. He's shaking."

"Marcus, I swear to you, I am hurting the Underdog as little as I possibly can." He continued to tend to Castor as he spoke, his movements careful and quick. "The venom in his system still poses a serious risk, so we need him conscious. That means I can't give him any more pain meds, unfortunately."

He's just trying to help me, Castor repeated to himself. As distrustful as he was of humans—especially anyone with a whistle—he definitely needed help now. And this human had always seemed kind. Deja's bites had left Castor in pretty rough shape. His muscles were still twitching a little, but at least the seizures had stopped.

"The fight looked bad, but so did the one before it, with the Enforcer and the Swift. I was surprised when neither one of them was really hurt, so I was hoping it was going to be the same way with this guy—mostly fake. No such luck." Pete shook his head and carefully tied off the thread, studying his handiwork. "I just can't believe he kept fighting after he was bitten," he said.

That's how a dog would fight a snake, Castor thought. *Valiantly.* Not that Deja turned out to be any ordinary garden snake.

"I told you he was special," Marcus said. He reached out and stroked Castor's ear with one hand—the other was still held to his chest by a sling of fabric. The boy was injured just like him.

Maybe that's why he had so much sympathy.

"Special or not," said the medic, "after that second bite . . ." He shook his head in disbelief as he dabbed the rotten skin on Castor's paw with disinfectant. "He's lucky he didn't lose that leg."

Castor breathed a sigh of relief. He was in bad shape, but at least he'd be able to walk with all four legs again. Or, perhaps more important, run.

Castor heard footsteps over by the entrance. Marcus dove back under the table, and Pete froze. Another man peeked his head around the doorway, but all Castor saw of his face were two dark, squinty eyes floating above a blue paper mask and below a blue paper cap.

"Pete? Did you call me?" he asked, and Pete shook his head no. "Weird. I thought I heard you talking to someone."

The young medic shifted on his stool. "I, um, was just finishing up in here."

The other Whistler didn't answer, but Castor could hear the shoes squeaking on the floor, and the sound was fading. The man was walking away.

Marcus hopped back up almost as soon as he'd left.

"Time to change the dressing on that schnozz," Pete said, gathering his tools.

When Pete removed the gauze, the exposure to air made Castor's snout a little tingly. But then, when Pete used forceps to dab at it with an alcohol-soaked cotton ball, it was a lot more than a tingle. Castor let out a wrenching groan of agony.

"You okay?" Pete asked. But he wasn't looking at Castor. Over the rims of his glasses, Pete was eyeing the boy as he backed away from the table.

The boy nodded, but then he stumbled into a swinging light, making a clatter. It helped Castor to focus on the boy instead of his nose.

"Are you sure, Marcus? You look sort of green."

Marcus nodded. "Just a little dizzy." He put his hand against a wall for support.

"How about you go to the training center for a bit?" Pete stood up, ushering the boy toward the door. "If you're caught, it's probably better than you being in here, anyway. You remember where it is, right? I'll finish up here and come meet you."

When Marcus left, Castor whined. He couldn't explain it, but he felt an odd connection with the human boy. Marcus made Castor feel a little calmer, and he already missed the gentle scratches behind his ear. Now there was just the smell of antiseptic, the bright lights, and the medic delivering good intentions with a side of pain.

"Easy, buddy," Pete said. "Just a little while longer, I promise."

31

Vince had come through, just like he promised. With Vince vouching for them, Leesa and Antonio had breezed right through NuFormz security, and now they got to stand outside of the gym's fence, where they could see some of the animals training. Leesa peered between the machines and scanned the rafters for the shimmery glint of a web, but she knew this was the wrong place to be looking for Pookie. Only the active fighters would be training, and the Chihuahua-spider was technically retired.

"Pretty sick, right?" Antonio asked, beaming.

Leesa watched a mutant bear smashing its skull against the back wall, over and over, in time with the mens' whistles. Just the sound of it was giving her a headache.

"Sick," Leesa repeated, but to her, the word meant something totally different. She wanted to leave this room and check out the rest of the facility, but they had to wait for Antonio's brother. Leesa looked toward the glass door of the office, where Vince was meeting with the supervisor. Vince's arms were crossed over his chest, and he was shaking his head.

"I don't care what she wants," he was saying. "He's not getting involved." Vince didn't yell, but he had the kind of voice that carried. Leesa thought she heard her friend's name somewhere in there, and Antonio must've heard the same thing, because he snapped to attention. With the whistles and the grizzly's banging, it was tough to make out much more of the conversation, but the supervisor's face was getting redder and redder.

"I can't believe your brother is friends with that guy," Leesa said.

"They're not like *buds*," Antonio said defensively. "It's business."

Leesa rolled her eyes. That man was one of the people

who took Pookie. Did it really matter what it was?

"You're the one who asked to come," Antonio grumbled. "Or demanded." Leesa could still hear the resentment in his voice. "I brought you to the island because I wanted to show you something cool, and you totally ruined it."

Leesa was aghast. Antonio was supposed to be her best friend, and he, above all people, knew what Pookie meant to her!

She was eight when her Chihuahua had first disappeared. Her family still lived above ground level back then, but when Leesa couldn't find her dog anywhere, she'd snuck down into the Drain. Most of the kids laughed at the dumb sky girl looking for her lost pet, but Antonio hadn't laughed. Instead, he'd led her through the dim, winding pathways of the sewer city and up into the Dome, and he'd shown her a whole new world: the world of the Unnaturals.

Pookie had eight new legs and a new name. It broke Leesa's heart to see him that way, but it was better than not seeing him at all. When she wanted to see the Poisonous perform, it was Antonio who had taken her to her first match, and to every match after that, sitting beside her for support as Pookie was beaten down again and again.

"How can you be so selfish?" she asked. "After all these years, I finally have a chance to find Pookie, and you're mad I wouldn't come see some stupid bridge?"

"Seriously, Leesa?"

The way he said her name sounded loaded—like there were a hundred unspoken sentences crammed into those five letters. Leesa looked at Antonio questioningly, and he sighed.

"I mean, come on. How can you still think . . . ?"

He didn't say anything for several seconds, but Leesa could feel her hands getting sweaty and her anger building before he'd finished the sentence.

"What? How can I think what?" Leesa glowered at him, daring him to say it: *How can you still think he's alive?*

She knew Antonio thought that if they hadn't seen Pookie in months, it was unlikely he'd survived. That there was no way Mega Media would keep an Unnatural around after he stopped fighting. That the idea of retirement or release was a joke in a place where they'd let the Invincible do what he'd done at the Mash-up.

Leesa knew Antonio thought she was irrational and naïve and stupid for having any hope. But she couldn't just give up, could she?

Finally, Antonio shrugged awkwardly, his hands

shoved deep in the pockets of his jeans. "How can you think that what happens in those stories is real?" he said instead. He reached for the book that was sticking out of her messenger bag and started paging through it, shaking his head. "Do you actually believe that anything will work out for the best? That's not how the world works."

That hurt more than anything Antonio could've said about Pookie. Leesa's eyes stung, threatening tears, but she blinked them away stubbornly. Leesa was not a crier, and she wasn't going to start now. Especially not in front of Antonio.

"I'm leaving," Leesa said in a huff.

Antonio started to protest, but she snatched the book from him. "No, it's stupid. Pookie wouldn't be with the active fighters in the training area, anyway."

She stuffed the book into her messenger bag, flung the strap over her shoulder and, flushed and furious, turned sharply on her heel, striding away from Antonio. . . .

And straight into someone else.

32

"OOF!" HE SAID WHEN THEY COLLIDED, AND LEESA'S BAG tumbled to the ground, sending her belongings scattering every which way.

"Watch it!" Leesa shouted. She knew it had been her fault, but her argument with Antonio still simmered just below the surface and made her bristle with new annoyance as she gathered up her things.

"Sorry," the boy replied automatically. "I didn't see you there."

His accent and his tone seemed too careful for the Drain, which made Leesa look up.

The kid looked about the same age as Leesa, and he was paler than anyone she'd ever seen. And though his white-blond hair was shaggy and hung in his eyes, his hoodie was brand name, and the skateboard he carried was all polished and expensive looking.

The boy saw her staring, and stared right back at her with bright, curious blue eyes. Leesa felt herself blushing, but before she could say anything, Antonio had sidled up beside her.

"Who's this clown?" he asked with a mocking laugh. "What are you doing here, sky boy?"

"I, um . . . am just here to get my arm looked at," the kid answered.

He nodded toward his sling, and Leesa noticed he had scrapes on his other hand, too, and a gash on his face. Probably from the board.

"My brother's a medic here."

"Well, my brother is Vince Romano." Antonio jutted out his chin. He was doing his stupid aggro act—wide stance, arms crossed over his chest.

"Okay," the kid said. He was smaller and looked a little wary, but he didn't shrink back from Antonio like some other kids did. "Good for him, I guess?"

It wasn't a challenge—the kid just seemed confused. Antonio, naturally, was not amused.

"It means he's the king of the Drain, sky boy, and if you knew anything about anything, you'd show a little respect."

"Antonio, relax." Leesa sighed. She was suddenly embarrassed and wanted to melt away. Antonio could be a ton of fun, but to most people, he must seem pretty intense.

The boy wasn't into comparing cred, though. He looked exhausted and preoccupied with something else. "Look, I'm not here to bug you, okay? I'm just waiting for my brother. You can go back to watching innocent animals get tortured or whatever," he muttered.

"I'm not a Moniac," Leesa snapped, offended at his accusation. "I'm just here looking for my lost dog. Let me know if you come across a giant mutant spider."

"You mean the Poisonous?" the sky kid gasped. "As in the Australian funnel-web spider and long-coat Chihuahua mix who had a win/loss ratio of twenty-four to six, the third best in the league, ever?"

Leesa raised an eyebrow. This kid was really geeking out.

"Sorry," he said with an awkward cough. "It's just that he was the only Unnatural to ever come close to

214

defeating the Invincible, which is a pretty big deal."

"So *you're* a Moniac." Leesa sneered at him disgustedly. "I bet you've never even seen them get hurt. Guys like you don't have the guts to sit through the real thing. You just warp in on fancy little screens."

"Big screen," the kid corrected. "But I don't anymore, now that I know what goes on." He glanced into the training area, and Leesa thought she saw him wince a little each time the whistle blew, just like she had. "Now I'm trying to save them."

Leesa could almost feel Antonio's disdain, but she couldn't help asking, "How?"

"I was trying to think of ideas . . ." Marcus kicked at the fence with his skate shoes, nervous to be put on the spot. "Like, I don't know, we could raise money to release some of them. Offer enough to buy their freedom."

Antonio's laughter sounded as sharp as the trainer's whip. "Who's got money to spare? You? Go back to your cloud castle. That's not how the world works," he repeated.

Leesa hadn't had an answer to that, but the sky kid did.

"Well, it should," he said. "And maybe if we try to do something, then one day, it can change."

"Nothing changes," Antonio practically spat.

The sky kid shrugged. "Some things do." Then he waved to his brother, who'd just come in the door, and dropped his skateboard. He turned to go, but first he gave Leesa a final, meaningful look and said, "I did."

33

Castor was left in the care center for the night to recuperate. The bed they gave him felt like a puffy cloud compared to the mat in his cell, and the medicine made his body so numb he nearly forgot his injuries. But though the pain from the fight was fading, the panic remained. Whenever Castor dared to close his eyes, he saw Deja's fangs, her head darting to strike, so long after the lights were shut off and the sound of human voices left the hallway, he lay wide-awake.

"How are you doing, pup?" a voice said in the darkness.

He hadn't even heard Pookie come in. There seemed to be nowhere in the facility that was off-limits to the old mutant.

"I've been better, to be honest," he answered. "Now I understand why they named me the Underdog. I barely had a chance."

"But you won the match!" Pookie said excitedly. "And you also won the loyalty of every fan in that stadium. As for your flying, it will get stronger."

The praise from his eight-legged mentor was a rare gift, and Castor couldn't help feeling a swell of pride. Still, he was wary.

"I don't think I'm up for training, if that's why you're here."

"Not tonight," Pookie told him. His mentor's voice was softer than usual, sympathetic. "I brought you something for comfort."

Castor heard a click as Pookie flipped a switch, and the overhead lamp snapped on, filling the room with greenish light. When Castor's eyes adjusted to the brightness, he saw that Pookie was holding out a strange, rectangular object. He set it on the bed in front of Castor's nose.

"What is it?" Castor asked, studying the picture on the front. It was surprisingly simple and antiquated, with no 3D imaging or interactive features.

"It has stories inside," Pookie said vaguely.

"About the ancestors?" Castor had never heard of stories being written down. Wasn't that what elders were for, to tell you about the past?

"Not just about the ancestors," Pookie said. "About make-believe things, too, I think. And about places you've never been."

Like the Greenplains.

As tired as he was, this was a subject Castor was definitely interested in. "Where did you find this?" he asked, adjusting his body so he could look up at his mentor.

Pookie's eyes were bright. "Leesa brought it," he said breathlessly.

"Leesa?"

"My human." Pookie sighed. "She was here today, watching your team in the training center. This fell from her bag."

His human? Castor couldn't fathom choosing to spend time with a human, knowing what they were capable of, but there was something about the wistful look on Pookie's face that made Castor want to know more about his past.

"You lived with her in the Sky Towers?" That was where most of the minis had started out—tiny dogs for tiny spaces.

Pookie nodded. "We were the best of friends from the time she was a little girl."

Man's best friend. That's what the Gray Whiskers had called the bond between humans and dogs. It was hard not to scoff. Some friend this human must've been for Pookie to end up here. She'd probably abandoned him on the street like so many others had when automopooches became popular.

But Pookie's pointed grin was wider than ever as he swayed slowly on his feet, remembering his time with Leesa.

"We did everything together. I sat by her side when she studied and lay in her bed while she slept. She's the one who taught me to do tricks."

"You learned all those flips and twists from a human?" Castor asked in disbelief.

"Not quite," Pookie said with a chuckle. "Back then we worked on simple things like 'roll over' and 'sit pretty.'"

Castor raised a furry brow and cocked his head. "'Sit pretty'?"

Pookie crouched on some of his back legs and picked up two of his front ones, holding them bent close to his chest. His expression was eager, and his tongue hung out of the side of his mouth. He lifted his chin and held the pose. "Sit pretty!"

To Castor it looked like a ridiculous version of begging, but if that's what humans thought was "pretty," he'd keep that in mind.

"You miss her?" he asked, watching Pookie from the medical bed. "That human girl?"

Pookie dropped his legs back down, and the action seemed heavy, though his delicate feet made no more than a whisper against the floor.

"I miss Leesa very much." The old dog smiled, but his voice sounded unbearably sad. "In truth, it's the only reason I still wear this old thing." He tugged at the collar around his scrawny neck. "Because it reminds me of her."

Castor was about to interrupt here—how he longed for the choice *not* to wear a collar!—but Pookie continued talking about the girl, his eyes wistful.

"I miss Leesa's voice and her scratches under my chin and the way she used to call me with a whistle." When Castor wrinkled his nose, Pookie explained, "Not like the Whistlers' whistle. It was a bright, happy sound she made with her mouth—a secret code between us. Sometimes I'd hear it in the stands during my matches and know she was watching. Leesa was the reason I tried to

221

win—I didn't want her to see me get hurt."

That made Castor think of Runt. He wouldn't want his little brother to see him in bad shape, either. Still, with his swollen nose and bruised leg, Castor looked worse than he ever had, and if his brother had been here, in the NuFormz prison, he would've run straight toward him, howling a hello. It also strangely made him think of the young human boy.

"Why didn't you go to her today, when you had the chance? Maybe she could've taken you home!"

Pookie shook his head. "I am no longer just her dog. It's better for her to forget me. This is my home now." His beady eyes drifted to the white walls, the waxed floors, the light that hung from the low ceiling, casting eerie shadows each time it flickered.

"I don't want to think of home right now, though. I want to think of somewhere else." His gaze snapped back to the book lying in front of Castor. "I never learned to interpret the humans' strange symbols, but there's a rumor that you might know how?"

Castor had felt so ignorant and useless in this place, but for the first time, he felt important. Pookie needed him now, and Castor was eager to help. He nosed the cover open, pointed his claw under the first line to mark his place, and began to read.

34

When Castor returned to training, Team Scratch greeted him with cheers all around the Pit. He was still limping on his leg a bit, and the wound on his nose had turned into a tender scar, but Castor felt safer than he'd expected to among these animals. Deja had been sneaky and cruel, and she slithered off to the other side of the Pit with Rainner. But looking at the concerned faces of Jazlyn, Moss, and even ornery Enza, Castor knew they had his back.

The grizzly-tiger ambled over, ready for her specialty: giving orders. "You're on flying duty today," Enza informed him.

When Castor grimaced—he hadn't flown since that night with Deja—Enza actually looked vaguely apologetic.

"You can take it on the easy side, but I want you off the ground. Samken choreographed a stellar routine for your match against him coming up, and we both want you to feel comfortable and know exactly what to expect."

"I guess I can do that." As much as he hated flying, he was grateful to just have a routine he could rehearse, and since his wings hadn't been injured, they actually felt stronger than a lot of other parts when he tested the muscles with quick stretches.

"Swipe, swipe, swipe!" Enza was directing Jazlyn now. The rabbit-panther was swatting at the air on the grizzly-tiger's command. "What is that? Do you plan to give them a pat on the head?"

"Teamwork is not about negativity, Enza," Moss reminded her.

"I'm not being negative!" the grizzly protested, but the next time Jazlyn hopped by, shadowboxing, Enza said, "That's better. Way more feline," and even batted playfully at Jaz's fluffy cottontail as she passed.

Moss flashed Castor a square-toothed grin. They were starting to feel like a real team after all.

That feeling changed later that afternoon, though, when Laringo's trainers had to drop off something at the office, and they parked the private transport truck right outside the Pit. It was bright red, and its sides were painted with elaborate images of the Invincible mid-strike.

All season, they'd only seen his poster glaring down at them as they trained while the whispered threat of last season's Mash-up stayed in the back of their minds. The handlers had been keeping Laringo from them until they were more seasoned fighters. *Or more worthy victims,* Castor thought as he folded his wings uncomfortably.

Enza stopped ramming her punching bag and drew in a sharp breath. "Do you think *he's* in there?" she asked, her gruff voice softened by wonder.

There was a loud bang in response, and then another, and then the whole vehicle started to shake.

Moss was shaking, too, but in a different way: from snout to hoof, the striped bull was the picture of fear.

"Enza!" the veteran neighed sharply. "Don't go near there!"

"It's Laringo!" she breathed with awe. She dropped down to all fours and eagerly lumbered over to the fence.

A white-striped face suddenly filled the window behind the bars, and immediately goose bumps crept over Castor's whole body, and next to him, Jazlyn shivered.

Unlike the flat blue eyes in the poster, the eyes that stared out at them were paralyzing. They were hyper-focused. Pale as ice and electric blue. And above all, consumed by utter madness.

Castor had seen rabid dogs before. Dogs that gazed into the distance but that couldn't seem to see. Dogs that couldn't quench their undying thirst. Laringo's stare held the same horrors, but Castor could tell that Laringo's rage didn't come from the kind of sickness that makes a dog rabid. It came from humans. Only humans could take a creature and transform it into something so unfeeling. The humans had tried to do it to Castor and he'd bitten his handler. Transformed, embattled, and beaten down, he was far from the scrappy street dog who'd entered the NuFormz facility weeks ago, but Castor knew his heart was still true.

As Castor looked into Laringo's cold gaze, he was grateful that he was learning to fight—not in the ring—but for himself. Even without giving them a look at his deadly tail or his slicing claws, with a single glance, the Invincible had managed to put every animal in the Pit on high alert.

Except Enza. She seemed enthralled by his power.

"I just want you to know, I wanted to be on your team from the beginning," she called out to him.

Laringo stared at her with those terrifying eyes, but he didn't speak.

Enza had enough to say for both of them, anyway. "I followed you from your very first match." She clutched the chain fence in her big bear paws as if trying to pull Laringo closer.

Laringo stared unblinking.

"Then I left the zoo because they didn't appreciate me, didn't respect me, and I knew I could be better. Stronger. Like you."

"You are not like me." When the Invincible finally spoke, his voice was not the booming growl Castor had expected, but rather soft, like velvet.

Enza chuckled awkwardly. "Well, I know I can't be exactly like you. There is only one Laringo—I get that. But maybe we could be friends and—"

"You don't want to be like me," Laringo corrected.

Castor could swear he heard a bit of desperation in Laringo's voice, but this was a champion. It could be that his speech patterns were just erratic—as if he were speaking a different language from his native tongue.

"Of course I do," Enza insisted. "We're already really

alike. For one thing, we're both tigers. Second cousins actually." She twitched her orange-striped tail as if to show proof. "I know we'll have to go against each other in the match tomorrow, but once we finish the season and we're both winners, we can be together and—"

"If we fight, you won't win." It wasn't up for debate. "Not unless Master says so. If we fight, you will not even survive."

Enza's gushy enthusiasm faltered. "Sorry?"

"You don't want to be like me, but you have to be like me to win and keep winning. I dream about fighting. Tonight while you lie awake, I will dream about killing you." There was no emotion in his voice whatsoever. It stayed soft and steady, as if listing what he had eaten at his last meal.

There's a reason he's not among us, Castor remembered Moss saying. *He'll murder us over breakfast.*

Enza blinked, the horror on her brown, furry face plain. Then she fell back hard onto her rump, and the giant she-alpha seemed to shrink into herself.

Laringo continued to stare her down until his handlers returned and started up the truck. Then, as it started to roll away, he called to Enza in a voice neither taunting nor cruel but scary all the same, "See you at the match."

35

Back in Castor's cell that evening, he was just set-tling himself in for a couple of hours of sleep before Pookie arrived for his lesson, when he heard a noise—a sort of yowling. At first, Castor thought it was some new training method Pookie had cooked up to catch him off guard, but then he realized it was coming from the neighboring cell.

He walked closer to the shared glass wall, the fine hairs in his ears twitching keenly. Castor heard the yowling again, along with some sniveling and whimpering and a fair bit of anguished howling.

"Enza?" Castor asked, not quite believing those sounds could be coming from the tough, quick-tongued giant. "Is everything all right?"

"LEAVE ME ALONE!" Enza roared fiercely from the corner. Her face was turned away from him, and Castor was grateful he couldn't see her maw of curving teeth.

"You got it!" he barked back.

So much for trying to help.

He was headed back to his deflated sleeping mat, but then the mewling started up again. Castor thought back to the conversation he'd had with Jazlyn once, about how everyone needed a break sometimes.

"Enza, I'm worried about you. What's wrong?" Castor asked again. If she really didn't want to talk, the worst she could do was hurl a few barbed insults his way and bang on the glass wall.

This time, the grizzly-cat tearfully opened up. "It's just that Laringo was my idol and he was so, so different from I thought." Enza hiccuped.

Castor thought of Laringo's emotionless eyes, his monotonous voice, and shivered. Now didn't seem like the best time to mention the fact that Moss had warned her repeatedly about Laringo's true, sinister nature, so

Castor kept his mouth shut and waited for Enza to continue.

"I'm different, too, I guess." She sniffed. "The Whistlers took my stripes and my swagger, and the bones in my throat, so I can't even purr. I'm barely even a cat anymore." She curled her long tail up and stared at it forlornly—the last sign of her old identity. "I'm worthless."

"Come on, Enza, you know that's not true," Castor said. "Besides, you've got other things now, like your teeth! You're the only animal in the world who has sabers."

"And a lisp . . . ," she complained, though to Castor, her speech sounded nearly perfect.

"Didn't you want to change, though?" Castor said as gently as possible, but he was getting a little impatient. It seemed like Enza didn't want to be comforted; she just wanted to feel sorry for herself. "I mean, I thought you came to NuFormz on purpose."

"Sort of." Enza shrugged. "In the big-cat exhibit, I was the only tiger. The other cats were always talking about how Laringo had made it big, teasing me and asking why I wasn't famous yet. Laringo's face was on the plastic cups from the zoo food stand. He didn't even come from the zoo, though—I'm pretty sure he was raised in the circus or the lab. I'd never met one of my own kind before. I lived with the other cats but never really had a pack like you. Somehow, Laringo's fame made him feel like I knew him. Like I was connected to something."

Enza finally turned from the corner, shifting her weight so she could look at Castor. She scooted closer to their shared wall and he leaned forward to hear the story.

"We didn't get very many visitors because we weren't as cool to kids as the mutants, but sometimes we'd get school groups. And sometimes, if the children were big Unnaturals fans, the zookeepers would point at me and say that I could be the next Laringo. I liked that—the other cats called me 'Hippo Butt' and stole my territory, but someone thought I could be a champion!"

Enza's eyes shined at the memory.

"So one day, when the zookeeper got to that part of the tour, I played along."

"That's when you scratched the girl?"

"All I really did was snarl," Enza scoffed, but when she looked at him, her eyes were earnest. "And it was just pretend, Castor, like we've been doing in training. Mimicking Laringo."

Castor thought of Enza that first day in the cages,

before they'd transformed. All catty confidence and extra swagger, he'd thought she was an alpha for sure. But maybe the tough tigress had been an act all along.

"I believe you."

"Yeah, well, the teacher didn't," she said with a quiver in her voice. "She threw a tantrum and I ended up here. Where there's no fresh meat, no fake grass or hollow boulders to stretch out on, no zookeepers to toss balls of yarn for you to play with. . . ."

The zoo wasn't exactly sounding like the awful place she'd hinted at. Castor was getting the picture now.

"I thought I'd at least have a friend in here."

Castor cocked his head at the slight. Was he not sitting here in the middle of the night, trying to cheer her up?

"I thought that with Laringo, I could meet another tiger. That I really could be a champion. But he hates me." Her shoulders started to shake again, and the tears returned. "And he's probably gonna kill me in the match tomorrow. I'm just this weak teddy bear and—"

Castor guffawed, and Enza's puffy eyes narrowed.

"How is this funny?"

"I'm sorry, Enza," Castor said. "But you are the last thing in the world from a teddy bear. Trust me, you're terrifying."

"Really?" Enza sniffled, a hopeful lilt in her voice.

"Oh, yeah. That first day I saw you, I thought you were going to bust right through the bars and tear me in half."

Enza cracked a small smile, and Castor took her silence as his cue to go on.

"And you know everything about hunting and pouncing—I've seen you train our whole team—so just because you have brown fur instead of stripes doesn't make you any less of a tiger than Laringo. Did you see those dead eyes? He's probably half robot."

Enza snickered in agreement. "He's basically an auto-mopooch."

"Only he's way less fun than the posters promised," Castor pointed out. "Someone should ask for their money back."

The grizzly was laughing hard now, and she slapped her bear paw against the back wall to steady herself. She must've hit it full force, though—it sounded like the cement was crumbling.

"Uh-oh," Enza said ominously.

"What?"

"The, um, door opened."

This wasn't news. Doors were always opening and

closing around here, but Castor didn't realize they'd been talking so far into the night. "Is it time for morning slop already?"

"No. Not the Slop door or the Pit door, or even the Dome door. It's the last door."

"The one that's cemented shut?"

Castor was on his feet now. Nose pressed up against the glass, he strained to see the place Enza was gesturing at, but there was too much of a reflection, and it was hidden in shadow. Enza was walking back to her corner now, away from the strange open door.

"You're not going to check it out?" Castor was aghast.

She shook her head and settled back onto her bed. "Not unless some Whistler makes me. It's dark. And scary. And probably sealed for a reason."

"What if it could take you away from Laringo?"

"And what if it leads to something worse?"

Castor had an identical door in his room, still sealed up tight. If it were to open, he definitely couldn't resist exploring. But Enza knew about regret better than he did, and she was right about one thing—none of the other tunnels had led anywhere good.

"We should probably get some sleep, then," Castor said, knowing how unlikely that was—he'd be craning his head at the mystery door all night. He flopped down onto the shredded remains of his blue mat, anyway, and sighed. "Big day tomorrow."

"Yeah . . ." Back in her corner, Enza's voice sounded small. "Would your friend have any tips for me when I fight Laringo?"

"My friend?" Castor asked, hearing the guilt in his voice.

"The old one. I hear you talking sometimes," she explained. "Don't worry—I won't say anything."

Castor was torn. Pookie had explicitly told him to keep his existence a secret. But Enza needed his help. Without specifically mentioning Pookie, he repeated the first thing his mentor had taught him, the truest thing. "Remember who you are," he told her. "It worked for me."

36

"WELCOME BACK, MONIACS! WE'RE ALREADY UP TO THE second week in our newest unnnnbelievable Unnaturals season!" Castor heard the announcer's voice echo.

He took slow, shallow breaths, inhaling the musky scent of burlap and trying not to overheat. It was just like before—the jostling by the handlers, the sack over his head, the dull roar of the crowd as the elevator eased to a stop—and Castor was having a hard time not having a panic attack when he thought about his fight with Deja.

But this was going to be different. This time, a friendly face awaited him on the other side of the door.

"Next up, get ready for a flight to remember and an elephant who never forgets! The Underdog, one of Team Scratch's newest additions, is here to take on the towering Enforcer!"

The muffled announcement was his cue, and Castor got into position. He stepped back with his right legs for balance and readied himself into a crouch. Muscles quivering with tension, he waited for the signal. The doors swung open and his blindfold was torn off; the bell dinged . . .

And Castor froze.

They'd gone over this. They'd rehearsed the routine all day yesterday, so he'd know exactly what to expect. He was supposed to spring forward into the Dome, fierce and wild and looking every bit like the valiant fighter he had been on the dock that day in Lion's Head.

But when he heard that bell, Castor was brought right back to his last match with Deja. He saw flashes of her fangs, a blur of butterfly wings, a flick of the rattle. Her cold, merciless eyes. He'd thought that was going to be a friendly fight, too.

Castor felt a kick at his hindquarters, and a shove from Horace brought him back to the moment.

He wasn't sure how long ago Samken had thundered out of the opposite gate, but the octo-elephant was rounding past him now, and his friend must've seen the look on Castor's face, because he gave him a reassuring wink.

Castor let out a breath. It was fake. Just like with Jazlyn. He was safe.

The performance was on.

The big bull elephant stomped around dramatically across the arena, grunting in mock fury. Samken really knew how to work the crowd—by the time he finally started his solo stampede, he had most of them shouting his name.

Now it was Castor's time to shine.

Samken was about to charge a second time and, just before he hit the eagle-dog, Castor would suddenly take flight and wow them all.

There was just one problem: he'd spent most of yesterday flying as they rehearsed, and though his mind had the routine down pat, his wings appeared to be completely useless. The muscles were sore and stiff from overuse. Of course, Castor didn't discover this until the very last minute, when Samken was kicking up dust just a few feet away from him.

Instead of wowing the crowd with unexpected flight,

they stunned them with a head-on collision.

Castor was more stunned than anyone.

The full force of Samken's two-ton body had slammed into him and, for a minute or so, he was actually unconscious. When Castor opened his eyes again, three giant heads were hovering over him, and there seemed to be tentacles everywhere. If Castor squinted hard enough, he could make the three elephant heads come together.

"Castor, I'm sooo sorry." Fat tears were running down Samken's cheeks. "I didn't mean to do that at all. I thought you were going to fly, like we talked about! Why didn't you fly?"

"Tried . . . ," Castor wheezed. He was so dizzy he felt nauseated. "Can't . . ."

Then the buzzing sound started. Horace was pushing the red button.

"Don't—"

Samken's high voice turned into a gurgle as he was zapped, and Castor could feel the bump on his head pulsing with each charge of his collar. Once it stopped, Samken rolled his eyes, like they were still rattling around in his head.

"Oof. Is that what they meant by 'singing the body electric'?" Samken groaned. "FAME!" he bellowed. When Castor looked at him blankly, he rolled his eyes.

"Didn't they have music in those sad streets of yours? They did at my zoo. Come on, the fans await!"

A voice asked over the loudspeakers, "Will the Enforcer unleash his tentacled wrath on the Underdog, as he did on the Swift?"

Samken glanced up at the floating announcer woman. "We'd better get moving. Ready, Castor? Let's try it again, this time just like we rehearsed—I run, you fly."

Before Castor could even mumble an objection, the octo-elephant took off for a third pass around the arena. Castor felt like he hardly took half a breath before the ground under his feet shook with Samken's fast-approaching feet.

Castor couldn't survive another hit, and he couldn't stand another shock. He needed to get out of this Dome, and there was only one direction he could go. He heard Pookie's voice telling him, *Up!*

"Now!" Samken shouted a warning so they wouldn't crash again.

Ignoring the throbbing in his skull, Castor jumped as high as he could, snapping his wings out to the sides. This time, amazingly, they caught him. He was hovering, then flapping.

He was flying!

But thanks to the bump on his head, Castor couldn't

seem to remember where he was supposed to go. He swooped in awkward circles. He veered to the far edges of the Dome. He nearly crashed into the crowded stands. He might've been flying, but he was way off script.

Luckily, Samken was good at improv. Each time Castor careened over him, Samken acted like he was trying to jump up and grab him. And whenever Castor nearly dive-bombed into the sand, Samken kicked his feet up like he was about to be tackled at the knees. The result was a dancing, many-trunked goliath that looked like a circus clown and a flying dog that could've been a toy airplane running low on batteries.

The fans might not have been wowed, exactly, but they were laughing like it was the funniest thing they'd ever seen.

"'Fame! I'm gonna live forever,'" Samken sang under his breath as the humans stomped their feet on the tinny bleachers and cheered their approval at the end of the match. "'I'm gonna learn how to fly. . . .'"

The grand finale was Castor spiraling in circles, dodging Samken's flailing tentacles as the octo-elephant rammed into the arena wall and feigned a knockout.

Though Castor had escaped the Dome mostly unscathed after his match with Samken, he still had an egg-sized bump on his head that needed to be looked at. The medic strapped him to a gurney, but when he rolled him past the holding pen, Castor saw Laringo. He could see the tiger-scorpion's muscles quivering with tension beneath his stripes. His head was alert, his ice-blue eyes already glued on Team Scratch's door across the field, searching for his prey.

Castor's heart skipped a beat.

Enza's match was about to begin.

As Pete rolled him through a doorway, Castor bucked and barked and wedged his legs in the door so the gurney wouldn't move.

"Laringo!" he howled, trying to get the scorpion-tiger's attention from the other side of those high stadium walls.

He'd told Enza to remember who she was, and he wasn't sure if Laringo could do the same. But to break Laringo's concentration and give Enza any sort of fighting chance, it was worth a shot.

"Laringo, listen to me!" Castor barked insistently. "You told Enza she didn't want to be like you, but you can change. Think of the cub you were before the scientists, before the serum. Before the humans made you fight. You can go back to him, you can be the brave beast he would want you to be. You don't have to do this!"

243

But then the door closed in front of Castor, and the opportunity was gone. Laringo had to have heard Castor. But Laringo hadn't even turned his head. His cold, blue-eyed gaze awaited Enza.

37

As the Invincible stepped into the ring, Leesa held her breath. Last season's Mash-up was still a touchy subject, and you could feel the tension building in the Dome.

Everyone had been laughing and cheering together during the Underdog's match against the Enforcer, but now scuffles began in the stands, and howls of excitement had turned into snarls of unrest. Team Scratch and Team Klaw fans alike were out for blood.

That was one thing the Invincible could be counted on to deliver.

Today he was fighting the Fearless, and Leesa was worried about the newbie. Really worried. After seeing the majestic grizzly-tiger close-up, Leesa couldn't bear to watch her get torn apart.

Though the Fearless and the Invincible were both part tiger, it was by no means an even match. The younger mutant was heavier and stood taller, but the veteran had unrivaled speed and ferociousness, and a formidable track record that included a long list of deceased opponents.

Leesa knew she had the best seats in the house from up on the light post, but right now, she wished she could see less.

"This should be over quick," Antonio said.

Leesa ignored him. Things had been tense between them since that day in the training center. Lately, he seemed either deliberately cool or like he was trying to find new ways to annoy her. Today he'd brought jalapeño zingers and hadn't offered her a single one. She didn't care, though; her stomach felt too queasy from the match, anyway.

The bell sounded, and the Invincible was on the offensive from the very start.

He prowled forward with quick strides, his scorpion tail held high and ready to strike.

Across the arena, the grizzly had crouched her big body low to the ground. At first, it looked like a defensive pose, but as Leesa noticed the tense shoulder muscles, and the way the bear had risen on the balls of her broad hind feet, she realized it was actually an offensive position. The Fearless looked ready to pounce.

"She's not running away," Leesa whispered, leaning forward from her perch on the platform as the champion neared the center of the ring.

Almost all the Invincible's opponents tried to evade him for as long as possible, flying or galloping or slithering around the arena until time ran out. Few actually had the guts to face him.

The grizzly-tiger wasn't just going to hold her ground, either; now she was running to meet him.

"Maybe she really is fearless."

Beside her, Antonio shrugged. "Either that or just stupid."

When they clashed in the middle, they looked like two big cats batting at each other's necks and faces. Instead of playful cuffs, though, long claws tore and tusklike teeth gnashed.

The Fearless stood up on her hind legs, trying to

make the most of her height, but it just made it easier for the Invincible to swipe at her middle. The Fearless let out a ferocious grizzly growl, crashing forward onto four legs. The wound was deep—that was obvious from her shorter movements and wincing steps.

The Fearless tried to lash back at the white tiger, but her bulk made her too slow, and he was already behind her, his barbed tail stabbing forward over his head. When the stinger struck her shoulder, the sound the Fearless made this time was more howl than growl. She gnashed her giant saber teeth, but the pain on her face was obvious, and you could almost see her hopeless realization that her height and her sharp teeth were no match for the poison that laced the Invincible's stinger.

"She can survive," Leesa said aloud to reassure herself. "Like Pookie."

"Right . . . ," Antonio muttered.

"What?" Leesa jerked her gaze away from the dueling Unnaturals to look at him. She'd been so absorbed in the fight she'd forgotten he was even there with her. "Pookie had the guts to face the Invincible, too, and he survived," she repeated, annoyed. "We both saw that match, and we agreed it looked like he won, actually, no matter what the official call said. Remember?" She narrowed her eyes at him.

Antonio sighed. "I know what we saw." He ran a hand through his thick, wavy hair, reslicking it. "But it doesn't matter, Lees. They end up dead in the end, anyway, don't you see that? All these loaded cloud kids pay good money for it."

Leesa's jaw tightened, but she didn't answer him. Instead, she reached into her bag for her paperback from Ms. Hoiles, which had become a tactile reassurance when she was upset. She knew it was stupid and babyish, but just holding it close to her made her feel like Pookie was nearer somehow.

But it wasn't there.

"Did you move my book?" Leesa asked in alarm.

"Nope." Antonio shrugged, unconcerned.

Her talisman gone, and her hope fading, Leesa's empty stomach tightened with worry.

The Invincible had the Fearless pinned beneath him now, his white-striped paw pressed on the grizzly's throat. He raised his scorpion's tail up slowly behind him, the translucent membrane curling forward. Leesa couldn't be sure but Laringo seemed to be letting the grizzly-tiger lash at him, drawing out the last few moments of the fight for fun.

Why wasn't anyone doing anything?

Leesa looked around at the handlers and guards.

Everyone knew what the Invincible was capable of—they'd all been at the Mash-up. Why weren't they stepping in?

Up in the box seats in the upper balcony, she could see Mayor Eris through one of the glass windows—her long, burgundy hair was easy to pick out.

"She could stop it," Leesa said bitterly. "Instead, she's just sitting up in her box, watching the money roll in."

Antonio popped the last jalapeño zinger into his mouth. He looked amused, which annoyed her even more. "And what about you? You're always talking about how things need to change," she said bitterly. "But all you are is talk, just like everyone else."

"Don't worry, Vince and me are on it." Antonio flashed a mischievous grin and flicked a pocket lighter a few times while wiggling his eyebrows. "One day we'll blow all these sky dwellers up, just for you—a revolution!"

Leesa looked at Antonio uneasily. Lately, she couldn't tell whether he was joking when he said scary stuff like that—stuff that sounded exactly like something Vince would say. That was Vince's lighter, too, she noticed, watching the flame dance. She wondered when Antonio had started carrying it.

If only the Fearless had fire, Leesa thought, looking

back down at the ring. *Then she might have a way out of this match.*

Abruptly, Leesa stood up on the platform, struck by a sudden idea. She snatched her messenger bag, and Antonio looked at her quizzically.

"Come on!" she shouted at him, already climbing down the ladder.

38

EVER SINCE THE DAY HE'D SPRAINED HIS SHOULDER, AND Marcus had learned the truth about the Unnaturals, Pete had been helping Marcus come back to the facility to visit the animals without Bruce or his mom knowing. But this was the first time he'd gotten up the courage to watch a live match, and he'd picked a doozy.

It was even worse than he'd feared, and Marcus wasn't sure he could watch another second of this slaughter. He couldn't stand the meanness of it all, written on every cheering face. He shifted his gaze from the battle to the space high above the field, where Joni Juniper's avatar refereed, silently begging her to stop the match. He couldn't catch her eye, but when the stadium lights switched over to a spotlight on the two tigers, Marcus did see something else.

Someone else, in the strangest of places.

High atop one of the light posts, Marcus caught the sudden movement of a figure standing up. He commanded his simulink vision chip to zoom in and saw it was a girl. *The* girl—the one he'd met in the training center days ago, with the tan skin and smart eyes and strange intensity.

Though he definitely hadn't expected to see her tonight, she was the whole reason he was here. And now she was leaving.

Marcus watched as she climbed into a hole at the top of the post and disappeared inside. Then there was that guy from before, too—the bully—climbing down after her.

Marcus leapt out of his seat, too. He felt bad for leaving after he'd begged Pete to get him these tickets, but he'd seen enough. And he had to catch up with the girl.

Trying to protect both his hurt arm and his skateboard, Marcus pushed past other fans and their annoyed protests until he reached the aisle. Then he took the stairs two at a time and when he got to the bottom, he ran. He got to a maze of interior hallways, where he could no longer see inside the Dome, and he looked around, unsure which path to take.

Luckily, a sudden, loud siren answered his question.

Down the hall to his left, he saw them standing in front of the fire alarm, and they saw him watching. In the next instant, the boy was running. The girl stared at Marcus for a second, and then she took off, too, her long braid swinging behind her.

"Wait!" Marcus yelled, but obviously, there was no way they were stopping.

This is why you carry a skateboard.

He kicked hard and tore after them, his wheels spinning over the waxed floor so fast that the deck shook beneath his feet. His bum arm made him teeter a bit, but he was still gaining on the two kids. When they disappeared around a corner to the right, he pressed on his back foot to make the sharp turn, almost careening into the girl.

He reached his good arm out and caught her hand. Apparently, she wasn't expecting it, though. He heard her black boots skid on the floor, then she whipped around and yanked her arm away from him.

Marcus, already off balance, went flying off his board to crash and burn. The floor seemed a lot less smooth when your bare skin was dragging on it, and now his injured arm wasn't just aching, it was throbbing. Marcus groaned, and the girl's face appeared above him, her cool blue steak of hair dangling in her eyes.

"Hey." Marcus smiled, but the girl didn't smile back.

"Don't ever grab me like that," she told him, but despite the anger in her voice, it softened a little when she saw him cradling his arm. "You fall a lot, huh?"

She reached down to help him up, and Marcus felt pretty awkward, but he took her hand, hoping his own wasn't too sweaty.

"Sorry," he said when they were face-to-face. "I'm Marcus, by the way."

He waited for the girl to say her own name, but she shot Marcus a guarded look and crossed her arms. "Did you . . . follow me here?"

"What?" Marcus's face flushed. "No! I was in the stands. I had seats. I mean, my brother got me tickets. . . ." He must sound like such a lame sky kid right now. He knew how expensive Dome seats were, and he'd only gotten them because Pete had a hookup at work.

The girl glanced behind her at her friend, who was beckoning to her from down the hall.

"Anyway," he said quickly, before she could leave, "I saw you up on the light thingy, and I just needed to tell you that you were right."

"About you being a Moniac?" She raised a dark eyebrow at him questioningly.

Real smooth, Marcus.

"No. I mean what you said about me being a phony for not seeing the live matches."

After he'd learned the truth about the mutant animals, Marcus had gotten rid of all his most valuable Moniac cards and he'd stopped following the stats. He never wanted to see the Unnaturals fight again, but when the girl said he couldn't really understand how the animals felt without being with them in the Dome, he knew he had to do it. Just once.

"You were right. It's way worse being here, but I'm glad I came. And I'm really glad you pulled the alarm when you did."

The girl shrugged like it was no big deal, but he could tell she was proud. "Hey, if we do something, maybe things will change, right?"

Hearing his own words, Marcus beamed. He was about to ask her name, and what the Drain was like, and how she got up on that light post, and how she thought they could save the Unnaturals, and a million other things.

Instead, right then, the doors from the Dome banged open, and the crowd started to pour through them. Marcus could see blue lights flashing around the corner.

"Leesa, let's GO!" the older boy yelled, and pushed through the emergency exit at the end of the hall.

Then the wave of people closed in around him, and before Marcus could even reach for his skateboard, the girl—Leesa—was gone.

39

CASTOR LAY SPRAWLED ON HIS BELLY ON THE FLOOR OF his cell, his wings splayed limply behind him. His chin rested on his front paws, and he stared through the glass wall into Enza's empty room. The Whistlers were working on replacing the fourth door, and they'd cleaned the floors and walls. Yet there was no sign of Enza, and no telling whether she was coming back.

When the Whistlers carried Enza off the field after the loud bell ended the match, they'd taken her through a big red exit door at the back of the stadium, where they transported only the most serious injuries. Moss said animals almost never came back from the "Hurt Door."

She could be dead for all he knew.

Castor heard keys jingling in the hall, but he didn't even lift his head—it was just the medic, coming to check on the bump on his head. Pete was gentle with him, but Castor doubted he would've noticed if the man had been rough. His body felt as numb as his mind. All he could focus on was Enza's empty bed in the cell next door.

The medic saw him staring. "You're worried about her, aren't you, buddy? She had a rough go, but I think she's going to be okay thanks to the fire alarm." Pete chewed his lip like he did when he was thinking of breaking the rules, and Castor's ears perked up. "Maybe in a few days I can take you over to see her or—"

Castor jerked his head up and gave a sharp yip. He was alert now, his ears standing up, his eyes pleading. He pawed at Pete's leg.

"Or I could take you right now, I guess?"

Castor barked his appreciation, actually wagging his tail now. Pete clipped on a leash, and Castor bounded after him through the door. The medic was visibly nervous as they went through checkpoints on the way to the care center, but the halls were empty. The jingle of his keys and Castor's clicking claws were the only sounds in the maze of empty hallways.

Inside the little white room of the clinic, the giant bear was laid out on a gurney that took up most of the room. Her orange-striped tail hung limply off the end of it, and Castor would've thought she was dead if it wasn't for the awful rumbling sound her chest made with each breath.

Castor immediately ran to the gurney, stood on his hind legs to reach Enza's lolling head, and sniffed at her for signs of life. Enza opened her eyes and, despite her saber teeth, it almost seemed like she was smiling. Castor knew it wasn't possible, but he could've sworn he heard a purr.

"See? She's just a little banged up, like you were," Pete said with forced enthusiasm. "She'll be good as new in a few weeks."

But Castor knew the grizzly was in rough shape. Her head was wrapped in gauze, and where the fur on one shoulder had been shaved, the skin underneath was a mess from the scorpion sting.

"Hang in there," Castor told her. "Team Scratch needs you, Enza. Who else is going to make us run faster, jump higher, and train harder?"

In truth, Castor couldn't care less about training

anymore—what was the point? But he needed Enza to know she had friends. That was what she'd really wanted, after all.

"Time to change that dressing," Pete said, gathering his tools.

When the medic touched her, Enza's eyes squinched shut, and she let out a heart-wrenching groan. Castor whimpered himself, wishing he could help her.

"This is all my fault," he said, licking her face.

"No," Enza said, her breath heaving. "You said to remember who I was. But I didn't want to be who I was before, Castor. I didn't want to be scared and self-conscious, a follower. I wanted to be the tiger you saw in me. A huntress, a queen . . ."

She winced as Pete swiped a cotton ball over her wounds.

"You are," Castor said.

"I'm lucky the bell went off before he was finished with me," Enza shook her head sadly. "I should've gone through the fourth door when I had a chance. Anything would've been better than this. Promise me you'll go, Castor," Enza begged with shining eyes. "If you ever see an open door, promise me you'll run!"

PART THREE

FINAL FLIGHT

*"Big Cat Face-off Ends in Alarm Bells
and Death Knells!"*

"The Fearless Learns Meaning of Fear!"

*"Will Team Scratch's Underdog
End Underground?"*

40

Castor was up before the morning whistle. Even without his extra training with Pookie, he hadn't slept much. Enza's words kept replaying in his mind, but he didn't think he would wait for another door to open. *Now*, something in his gut kept insisting. Somehow, some way, they had to escape.

Castor trotted quickly down the tunnel, and burst into the slop room.

"We need to talk," he announced to the room.

Jazlyn jumped. She'd been jittery lately, and she could hardly have a conversation without bursting into tears.

The other animals barely looked up. Like him, they'd been walking around in a daze since Enza's match. There had been injuries all along, risks from the start, but this had been different. It had shown them the true darkness under those bright stadium lights.

"I saw Enza at the healing room, and Laringo almost killed her." His ears drooped, remembering her cries. "We've got to get out of here before something else happens."

"Brilliant idea, Castor," Moss said dryly. "Right after breakfast, let's all just strut through the checkpoints and right out the front door!"

The bull was red-eyed and touchy. He'd warned them that Laringo was dangerous, but he seemed more affected by Enza's grave injuries than anyone. Just looking at him, Castor could see the tension in his shoulders, the anger simmering just below the surface.

"That's not what I had in mind," Castor said. "But there must be another way."

Samken giggled, but Jazlyn nudged him to stop. "He's actually serious," she said softly. "Aren't you?"

Castor nodded. "We have to escape." Saying it aloud made him almost dizzy with hope.

The animals shifted uncomfortably, glancing at the door for approaching Whistlers. Submission had been so drilled into them that even the thought of freedom seemed taboo. Actually talking about escape was unthinkable. Moss nickered and turned away, not interested in hearing another word.

But others were curious and leaned closer over the trough.

Now Samken was looking at Castor with the determination he usually reserved for the arena, and his voice was dead serious when he asked, "How?"

Castor had been thinking about this all night. He still didn't have an answer.

"I'm working that out. But we'll think of something. Think of all the incredible routines we've come up with using each of our talents—we just need a plan." He spoke quickly, pleadingly, desperate to convince them. "If there was a way out, if we stuck together, I know we could make it."

"I think there's a door that leads out of the Pit," Jazlyn suggested haltingly. Castor glanced over at the rabbit-panther, thinking that she didn't seem quite herself, but he nodded his encouragement.

"That must be where Slim goes to smoke his paper sticks."

"The parrot patrols the Pit," Rainner noted.

"We could try the fourth door in the cells. . . ."

"The fourth door is s-s-sealed," Deja said with a flick of her forked tongue as she popped up by his side.

Castor tried not to flinch as he looked into her snake eyes. He'd tried hard to avoid Deja since the match, but she always seemed to be sneaking around where he least expected it.

Still, he wasn't deterred.

"The door in Enza's cell wasn't sealed. She gave it a little nudge and it just crumbled. I bet if we work on the others we can get them open."

"We don't even know where those tunnels lead . . . ," Jazlyn said anxiously.

Castor hadn't thought Moss was listening, but from down the trough, the zebra-bull answered, in a far-off, wistful voice, "They lead to the Greenplains."

Castor's jaw dropped, and his eyes grew wide. "The Greenplains are real?"

Since he'd arrived on the island, Castor had usually been exhausted from training, and he dreamt less and less of the mythical forest. It was like the features of Runt's face or the sound of his mother's voice: hazy and lost, part of a life he sometimes doubted had ever existed.

Now his memory of the dreams came back, stronger.

He saw the rows of strong trunks, the treetops reaching toward the sun. The haze of leaves wasn't just green, but many different colors—some closer to yellow or brown, some in shadow that made them seem blue or black.

"We had a view of the Greenplains from the Sky Zoo. You really didn't know about them?" Samken sounded surprised.

Deja didn't, either, but she'd come all the way from the desert. She darted her diamond head forward, keenly listening in.

"Unnaturals used to train there, but the land there is toxic," Moss explained. "That's why the Whistlers sealed up the doors."

"They've been cleaning it up for years, though," Jazlyn jumped in, eager to share her knowledge. "The children in my classroom studied the Greenplains, and the teacher was always talking about them as . . . what did she call it? 'A model for radioresistance and bio-hardiness in the post–Warming Age!'" She said it in one breath, like she couldn't get the words out fast enough.

Castor didn't understand any of that, but he knew what it meant. "There's a better life out there—right outside the door," he yipped.

"A life we can't have," Moss said.

"Animals have escaped before, though," Samken

reasoned. "I hear the chimps on the second floor chattering about it sometimes at night. There might be a whole bunch of Unnaturals who already made it to the Greenplains."

"They didn't," the zebra-bull insisted stubbornly.

"How do you know? They could be hunting squirrels right now. Squirrels and deer and fat birds!" Castor was so excited by the idea that he was barking as fast as Runt.

"I know because I was there!" Moss said sharply. "Because they were my teammates and I watched them try to make a break for it. I saw them run and I saw them caught by the Whistlers, and then I never saw my friends again."

"Maybe they were released, maybe they—"

"NO!" Moss ground his square teeth together and shook his horns. "I know, because that's why the Whistlers ignored the rules of the Mash-up and let Laringo kill all the Unnaturals from both teams. Everyone."

"Except you." Deja slithered across the concrete floor toward Moss. She lifted her diamond-shaped head and swayed in front of the striped bull and eyed him curiously. "You're s-s-still here."

Moss blinked at her. With his gaunt face and his deeply creased brow, the veteran coach looked old and broken.

"I'm still here," he repeated. "Because I hadn't tried

to escape. They wanted someone to remember. But the others, Firan, Buzzle, Pookie . . . they weren't so lucky."

Castor's ears twitched at the unexpected mention of his mentor's name. And suddenly, he was certain that giving the old bull hope was more important than keeping the spider-Chihuahua's secret. "Pookie's not dead."

Moss narrowed his eyes. "You've seen Pookie?"

"I, uh, I've been training with him sometimes. At night. He can slip through doors."

Castor felt guilty for revealing Pookie's secret, but the way Moss was looking at him made him feel guilty for having kept it so long, too. The veteran was staring at him in shock, his expressive eyes flashing everything from relief to pain to anger. It was making Castor pretty uncomfortable, so he turned to the others.

"So, what do you guys think?"

Rainner was the first to speak. "Maybe Castor's just afraid of losing. You're next up to fight the Invincible, aren't you? You want us to risk our lives so you don't have to face him."

"No, I don't want to face him. But we'll all face him soon enough. You really want to be fighting in here for the rest of your life?" Castor demanded, frustrated. "How ever long or short that might be? Don't you want to go home?"

"My home is across the big water and among the long, dry grasses," Rainner scoffed, his horn jutting forward. "If that's not where you're going, I'd rather take my chances in the Dome."

Castor knew that Rainner was the one speaking out of fear, but he saw that same anxiety reflected on each of his friends' faces. He watched his dreams of escape fizzling away.

"What about the rest of you?" Castor pleaded. "Jazlyn?"

"I'm with you," the rabbit-panther said immediately, surprising Castor. "I have to get out of here. I feel like I'm losing my mind in this place, like I can't get my thoughts straight." She shook her ears as if to clear her head. "Maybe it's from the shot last week. Did it make you feel funny?"

"Shot?" Castor repeated, puzzled.

"You know, the booster shot." Jazlyn looked around, but none of her friends' faces showed recognition. "We always got weekly shots when I lived in the lab, so I just thought . . ." She trailed off, and the room went silent, each animal imagining new horrors.

"This is why we have to leave!" Castor said. "We have no idea what the Whistlers are capable of."

"If you want to go, Castor, I'll follow," Jazlyn said.

There was a quiver in her voice, but her eyes were bright. "I trust you."

Castor's heart warmed with gratitude. Maybe they still had a shot. He looked at the friendly gray face at the end of the trough. "Samken?" The octo-elephant hesitated for just a moment, and Deja cut in.

"You s-s-shouldn't go alone," the snake said. "Give us a little time to think this over. Wait and s-s-see."

Castor had been betrayed by Deja before, but Samken was nodding eagerly, and though he saw the panic on Jazlyn's face at the mention of a delay, he knew it was better if they could all go together.

"Okay," Castor relented. "We'll wait and see."

41

MARCUS'S FAMILY ALMOST NEVER ALL ATE TOGETHER, since Pete lived in his own place and Bruce didn't feel he could unwind after a hard day's work if he had to worry about conversation between bites. This was a special occasion, though: Pete had brought a lady.

Not just any lady, either. *The* Joni Juniper, superstar match announcer. Helping to heal Unnaturals was great and all, but no wonder Pete kept his job at NuFormz.

"Well, I know Marcus here is certainly excited to

meet you," his mom said. "He's one of your biggest fans."

"Mom!" Marcus protested, almost choking on his food.

Bruce loved an opportunity to pile on more embarrassment. "He's had a crush on you for way longer than Peter, right, Marky?"

Marcus could feel his face flushing pink near the temples as the embarrassment lingered.

Fortunately, Joni was as gracious as she was at the matches. "Thank you," she demurred with a warm smile, her teeth blindingly white against her dark skin. As usual, she knew just what to say. "We certainly appreciate Moniacs in this industry. They keep us all in business, don't they?"

A short while ago, Marcus would've been giddy just to see her face on his warp screen. It was ironic that she was sitting ethereally across from him at their dining table now that his feelings about the Unnaturals were so different.

"I'm not a Moniac," Marcus corrected her.

It came out more defensive and bratty than he'd planned. Joni laughed easily, but Marcus sensed her discomfort.

"Oh! My mistake . . ."

"I mean, I was." He backpedaled. He needed her on

his side, not thinking he was some jerky kid. "I just don't think the matches are right anymore because they're so violent."

"Really?" Bruce raised an eyebrow. "That's news to me." He definitely looked suspicious. Marcus had consistently begged for warp tickets as his only request for holidays, birthdays, and any other time he could squeeze a promise out of his parents.

"I don't know how you do it, Joni," Marcus's mom said with a shake of her head. "Sitting through all those virtual fights."

"Umm, it's difficult sometimes," Joni admitted without correcting her. "But I saw enough dogfights in the alleys growing up to know that it's just the circle of life."

Marcus looked at Joni, disappointed. That was a cheap, rehearsed answer if he'd ever heard one.

"Were you raised here in Lion's Head?" Marcus's mom asked.

"My parents live at ground level," Joni answered with a nod.

"Oh?" Marcus's mom raised an eyebrow, and Marcus could practically see the wheels in her mind turning, calculating the risks of exposure, wondering if Joni had anything that was contagious.

"But recently, I was able to move into my own apartment." Joni flashed one of her winning smiles, and Marcus's mom relaxed.

"It's where I was hoping to move, in the 110s," Pete added, and now their mom looked absolutely alarmed.

"Seems like a fancy girl like you would want to aim higher," Bruce said to Joni. "The 100s are practically ground level these days."

"I like seeing what's going on at the baseline." Joni twirled a forkful of noodles and gave Bruce a tight-lipped smile. "I find it more interesting than having your head in the clouds."

There was a weird tension in the room that Marcus didn't quite understand, and no one quite wanted to acknowledge.

"If you really want to know what's going on, you need to get out of the hologram box and onto the actual field," he suggested, trying to steer the conversation back to the Unnaturals.

"It's funny you say that." Joni leaned forward over the table as if letting them in on a secret. "I actually first got into the industry by cataloguing biogenetic breakthroughs and misreported stats. I wanted to be a journalist."

Bingo!

"Maybe you could do an investigative piece about Mega Media!" Marcus suggested.

Pete's laugh was nervous as he tried to diffuse the conversation.

"Marcus, what are you talking about? Joni and I both work for Mega Media. You know that."

Marcus ignored his brother and went right on chatting with Joni. "Like, about how the Unnaturals are real?"

Bruce glanced at Pete, and usually Pete would look away, but this time he stared right back at Bruce. Marcus could almost see the air wiggling from the heat of his brother's anger.

"I . . . did know that." Joni's tone was still upbeat, but it was more careful. "I think a lot of people are aware of the reality of the business."

"Well, a lot of other people are blind to what's going on, like I was. But you can show them." He pleaded with her. "They'll listen to you."

Joni looked at her plate.

"Marcus, drop it," Pete warned, glaring at his brother from across the table. "Everyone is doing the best they can, okay?"

"All right. As long as everyone is doing the best they

can," Marcus said, unable to keep the sarcasm out of his voice. "As long as you're doing the best you can."

Pete said he cared about animals, that he wanted to help them, he'd even snuck Marcus in to see them, but he wouldn't even back Marcus up at the dinner table! How would he ever stand for something bigger? All because he was afraid of Bruce the Brutal.

"You're the worst of all, Bruce," Marcus said. He gripped his silverware tightly and glared down the table at their stepdad. "You're the one in charge of the team that's altering them!"

"I'm a scientist, you know that," Bruce said evenly. "We lost so many creatures to extinction, and now we're finally able to bring back parts of them that were lost when they died out."

"How honorable," Marcus practically spat. "To save lost species in order to whip them and whistle at them and make them kill on demand."

"Marcus . . . ," Pete warned.

Marcus knew he should check himself, but he couldn't stop, and his voice was shaking with emotion. "To keep them in what used to be prison cells and never let them see the sun."

"Come on!" Pete interrupted. But it was too late. Bruce was already wheeling on Marcus's brother.

"You took him to the NuFormz facility, Peter?"

"Bruce, I can explain," Pete said, putting his hands up.

"You took an eleven-year-old boy into an enclosed area with a high concentration of the world's deadliest creatures. You really think you can explain that? That's the last straw. You can work out the week, but then I'd better see your resignation on my desk."

Pete's jaw tightened in frustration. "Thanks a lot." He looked at Marcus like he'd betrayed him, and Marcus dropped his eyes. "Come on, Joni. We should go."

She nodded, her dark curls bouncing softly, and grabbed her coat. "Thank you all for a lovely meal," she said brightly, the network personality working hard to overcome the stress in her eyes as she looked around the table.

"Wait," Marcus shouted, knocking over his glass of powdered milk as he shot to his feet. He knew he should stop, but he needed to explain and to make them see. "You saw what happened with the Fearless, Pete," Marcus despaired. "If no one does anything, the Invincible is going to bury the eagle-dog at the next match." His voice cracked, and he wiped his eyes, too angry to be embarrassed.

Pete held Marcus's eyes for a moment and then looked at Joni, but neither of them answered. Pete took

Joni's arm and walked out, closing the door quietly behind him, and for a moment, there was just the sound of milk dripping onto the floor. Then, acting like nothing had happened, Bruce very calmly went back to eating his dinner.

All Marcus could focus on was the sound of the knife scraping across his plate.

Marcus's mom watched him chew for a minute and then suggested gently, "Is there something you can do, Bruce, hon? Maybe get this dog out of there for him, at least? Marcus never had pets when he was little, and we're tight on space, but we could probably fit—"

Bruce scoffed, almost choking on his food. "I'm afraid I don't have that kind of power."

Was he serious?

"You have a ton of power!"

Bruce held his temper, as usual, and spoke to Marcus like he was a five-year-old. "We're doing important work, Marky. Some sacrifices have to be made. You'll understand that better after a few days—you're grounded."

Trembling, Marcus stomped off to his room. He took out the Blink, knowing he should do any virtual surfing while he still had access. He needed to text Leesa.

After the match, she'd found Marcus on the simu-link network and contacted him to see if he had some

281

book she'd lost—she thought she might've dropped it in the training center when they'd first met. He hadn't seen the book, but they'd been texting ever since. Buoyed by Leesa's small act of defiance, they wanted to help more Unnaturals, or stop the matches completely.

Stepdad in denial. Brother's too chicken. We're on our own.

Seconds later, he received a response to his text, and seeing Leesa's words made him feel light-headed.

Time to put the plan in motion. Meet me at Greenplains Bridge. Saturday. 3:00 p.m.

42

"SHOULD WE START AGAIN FROM THE BEGINNING?" CAS-
tor asked when Pookie arrived, retrieving the book from
its usual spot hidden under his mat. Pookie was obsessed
with the story and insisted on reading part of it every
night before training. They had now finished the text a
second time, but Castor waved the book in his mouth
suggestively, hoping that Pookie would be eager enough
to read it that he wouldn't want to discuss certain other
things. . . .

But Pookie wasn't scuttling around the cell like he usually did and there was none of the characteristic playfulness on his face. Instead, his legs were flexed stiffly, and his black, beady eyes bore into Castor.

"You broke our contract," the mini said finally, his white whiskers quivering. "You were never supposed to speak of me."

Castor ducked his head apologetically. "I know, but—"

"You betrayed me!" Pookie snapped, and lifted his first four striped legs off the ground so that he stood tall and fierce, with his red fangs prominent.

It was the first time Castor had seen Pookie in an aggressive pose, and he cowered as if he'd been whipped. With his tail tucked low, he crawled toward Pookie submissively.

"I never meant to," he said in a soft voice, keeping his eyes on the floor and away from those scary fangs. "Moss was heartbroken thinking you'd died. I just wanted my friends to know we had a chance at freedom. You go anywhere you want in this place, and you don't follow anyone's rules."

Pookie sighed and dropped his legs back down, the benevolent mentor returning. "Escape was always easy for me but I have not found freedom." His voice was wary. "I thought I could help others escape, it's true." Pookie flexed his spider legs pensively as he started to tell the story. "I convinced both teams to join me—everyone but Moss. I cursed that stubborn bull at the time, but he was right. We barely made it out of the Pit before we were apprehended. And later, in the Mash-up, Moss's obedience was rewarded, and he was spared. I slipped through the cracks as usual. As for everyone else—" Pookie dragged one of his front legs across his own white, furry throat. "Dead, all of them." The Chihuahua's voice was a high squeak now, on the verge of breaking. "Because they believed in me."

"No," Castor said, trying to comfort his friend. "It's not your fault."

"It is!" Pookie barked, turning away. "And I was a coward and went into hiding. I've managed to avoid capture, slinking around the cells at night, stealing food from Laringo's private pantry. But as a fugitive, I am more trapped than ever."

"But you can still break out of here. Look." Castor went to the glass and pointed his nose toward Enza's cell, where part of the fourth door was still being repaired. "You don't have to settle for reading Leesa's book over and over to feel close to her. You can go home."

Pookie sighed again, and his wrinkled little face

looked older than ever. "No. What home can there be for a mutant? I am not the Pookie that Leesa once knew. I am not soft or small or snuggly. Neither are you, Castor. You're scary to the outside world. Like me, your home is in here."

"This isn't what I thought you were teaching me." Castor dipped his tail and his wings in dismay. "I thought you said I was still Castor. Just like you're still Pookie."

Pookie gently placed one of his legs on Castor's paw. As Castor looked into his mentor's eyes, he realized Pookie's muzzle looked grayer than ever and that the Chihuahua dog looked tired. Pookie guided Castor back into his training position, shutting down any further talk of escape.

"You must learn how to work the system, like we talked about. You're on the verge, young pup!" The encouragement was back in his voice. "Laringo can barely think for himself—he's completely controlled by the mayor—and if you can defeat him, you will be untouchable. You'll have the crowd on your side once and for all. Remember, when you have the fans, you have the Whistlers, including Mayor Eris."

He crawled up the wall so he was at Castor's eye level. "Now breathe in through your nose," Pookie directed. "Fill your chest up like a proud warrior. Now rise!"

Castor beat his wings and started to fly around the cell, his panic growing as every turn made it feel smaller and smaller. It was all metal, all locks, all bars. He didn't feel like himself or like a proud warrior or even a good faker. He felt like a trapped animal.

❧

A siren wailed, and red lights flashed.

"Alert! Alert!" the parrot was shrieking from the guard's desk. "Escape on the cell block!"

The animals were being herded to slop so that the guards could check each cell, and among the chaos, Castor instinctively glanced into the cell next to his to check on his friend. Enza wasn't there, of course—she was still recuperating in the care center—but Castor noticed something strange in her cell.

The scaly remnants of a snakeskin lay in a crumpled coil in front of the fourth door. *Deja,* he thought immediately. She must have had the same ability to squeeze under doors like Pookie. Yet unlike his mentor, she wasn't afraid to use it to leave the Dome. She'd been biding her time waiting for her moment. The snake had shed her life in this place and struck out first for a new one.

A green one.

It was a life that should've been his, but now the handlers were too watchful.

In the slop, the other animals were resigned.

"She told us not to trust her," Jazlyn sighed.

"Enza didn't from the beginning," Samken pointed out.

"We can still make an escape plan," Castor said desperately. Despite his talk with Pookie the night before, he couldn't let his hope die. Not yet. "We can still get to the Greenplains. . . ." Even now, he could almost smell the grass.

"The Greenplains is a dream, or it might as well be. It's too late," Moss huffed. The zebra-bull was agitated and pacing. "It's just like before. We're the ones who will pay for Deja's actions."

"But I'm supposed to fight Laringo," Castor whimpered. "If there's no hope for freedom, I don't know what I'm fighting for."

"That's nonsense." Moss looked at him sternly, a veteran of lost wars. Still, the bull's chocolate eyes burned into Castor's, insistent. "Every time you enter that Dome, you fight for yourself."

43

WHEN LEESA CLIMBED UP OUT OF THE DRAIN AND STEPPED onto the beach, she could see feet dangling off the bridge over the water, and she knew Antonio was already there. That was good—she'd have a chance to prep him before Marcus arrived.

She and Marcus had worked out every detail of the plan in advance: Marcus would get his brother's keys, but to avoid the eye scan checkpoints, Antonio could help them get in the back way through the training center. It should be empty at night, but Antonio could use Vince's name for credit if necessary. Then they'd unlock all the cages, herd the animals onto transport trucks, and drive them over the bridge to the Greenplains.

But no matter how airtight Leesa thought her plan was, she knew it was going to be hard to sell it to Antonio. He was so skeptical of everything these days, and if it involved keeping secrets from Vince or using his name, forget it. They'd waited until the day of the planned jailbreak to tell him so that if he agreed, he wouldn't have time to back out.

The Invincible's next match was tomorrow, so it had to be tonight. Before the scorpion-tiger had a chance to kill somebody else.

Leesa heard a buzz in her pocket and knew that was probably the sky kid, but she needed to talk to Antonio first. She took a deep breath as she made her way out to the middle of the bridge to join him.

"Hey," Leesa greeted him.

"Hi," Antonio said. When he looked back at her, his face looked sort of flushed, but she guessed that was from the sun—she could already feel herself burning in the midday heat.

Leesa stepped gingerly past the safety rail, and she was blown away by what she saw. From up here, the light looked like it was dancing on the river. She felt like she was floating.

"Wow. This is so cool." Leesa gasped.

Antonio smirked. "Didn't I tell you?"

The lush forest of the Greenplains was on her left, the towering metropolis on her right. "Even Lion's Head looks kind of pretty from here," she said.

"Everything looks pretty from here," Antonio agreed, staring up at her. "Even your chunk of blue hair." To Leesa, that sounded like an insult, and she tucked the blue strands back into her dark braid. But Antonio was smiling at her shyly.

"Antonio . . ." Leesa sat down on the ledge near him and cleared her throat. "I'm really glad you came. I need to talk to you about some things."

"You don't even have to say it," he said. "I know why you've been acting so weird with me lately."

Leesa blinked at him, caught off guard. She was acting weird?

"I figured it was probably nerves and that you were maybe a little insecure about it—which you don't have to be at all because I know you better than anyone." He scooted over on the ledge, closing the gap between them. "And I have to admit that I was close to giving up, but when I got your text I just knew that you finally got it, that you were ready."

Leesa had a funny feeling in her stomach, but she wasn't sure if it was from looking down at the water, or the hot sun, or knowing the mutant compound was so very close, or if it was Antonio who'd put it there.

"I want you to know that I'm ready, too."

"Ready . . . to help the Unnaturals?" Leesa asked, doubtful.

He actually laughed. "Ready to be together!"

Leesa's tablet buzzed again, and she started to reach toward her pocket, but Antonio darted his hand out and took hers, awkwardly threading their fingers. Leesa felt the clammy sweat from his palm. Then he started to lean toward her, smelling sickly sweet from the cologne he'd borrowed from Vince and splashed all over himself, and Leesa realized that feeling in her tummy was closer to dread than butterflies.

She slipped her hand out from under Antonio's and coughed.

"What's wrong?" Antonio asked. His dark eyebrows knit together with concern.

"Uh . . ." She coughed again. The polluted air was starting to get to her, making her talk all scratchy, but the words themselves felt like they were stuck in her throat. "Antonio, I—"

"What?" he asked impatiently.

I don't think of you like that. I want things to stay how they are.

But before she could say anything, the hollow sound of footsteps echoed up the bridge, and she and Antonio both turned toward the shore to see Marcus, dressed in a hoodie and long pants despite the high temperature, running at them full speed.

"What's sky boy doing here?" Antonio demanded.

"That's part of what I wanted to talk to you about. . . ."

"You invited that clown to our spot?" The confusion on Antonio's face quickly morphed into hurt, then anger. "Seriously, Lees? Look at him—he's wearing a gas mask!"

Leesa started to explain, but as Marcus got closer, she saw the alarm on his face.

"What's wrong?" she asked, standing up so abruptly that she almost pitched off the bridge.

"Didn't you . . . get my texts . . . ?" Marcus's mask fogged up as he tried to catch his breath.

Leesa shook her head, but she was already whipping the tablet out of her pocket.

Emergency! Call ASAP!

Underdog/Invincible match moved up.

She looked up at Marcus, her voice small. "When?" she asked.

He must've had one of those expensive, newsfeed chips scanner upgrades in his tablet.

"Four o'clock," he answered, and Leesa's heart fell. They had only twenty minutes.

44

MARCUS KNEW HE WAS IN BIG TROUBLE. HE WAS ALREADY grounded and to get to the bridge, he'd had to sneak out without his mom noticing and come into contact with pretty much everything he'd been taught to fear: midday sun exposure, proximity to both the toxic river and the Greenplains radiation that had killed his father, open air at ground level. . . .

He'd swiped one of Bruce's gas masks and used the money he'd been saving for a new skateboard deck to buy extra oxygen, and he'd been careful to check that none of his skin was showing. But Marcus still felt pretty anxious when he stepped out of a cable ride he'd hitched with strangers and crawled under a barbed fence on Reformer's Island. It was as he was picking his way across the slippery, moss-covered rocks, the base of the bridge finally in sight, that he'd gotten the update via simulink.

ATTENTION MONIACS: DUE TO HIGH DEMAND AND FAN FRENZY, THE MOST-ANTICIPATED MATCH WILL BE MOVED UP! THE INVINCIBLE WILL BATTLE THE UNDERDOG TODAY, WITH A SPECIAL SURPRISE TO BE ANNOUNCED!

"Why would they change the date of the match?" Leesa was distraught. "There's no way they'd get a packed stadium on such short notice, and this was supposed to be the biggest match of the season. It doesn't make any sense."

"None of this makes any sense." Antonio was in a thin, white tank top, and he crossed his arms over his chest.

Marcus shrugged. He'd learned from his dad's death that the worst things rarely made much sense, but you still had to find a way to deal with them. Antonio seemed like the kind of dude who might lash out when he was confused, though, so Marcus kept that bit of advice to himself.

"We had a plan to free all of the animals at NuFormz," Leesa explained to her friend. Antonio's eyebrows knit together and he looked like he was about to yell, but Leesa quickly added, "But it's ruined now that they moved up the eagle-dog's match."

Antonio's face relaxed, which really ticked Marcus off. This guy didn't even want to help the animals. He was relieved to be able to walk away from them. Now Marcus was more determined than ever.

"We can still do it," he insisted. He fished into a pocket in his pants for the jangling mess of metal, and thrust his hand toward Leesa. "I already took Pete's keys. There's a private exit door right on the side that I know my brother uses to get animals out quickly after rough matches. We won't be able to free all of the animals we wanted to, but if we get to the arena now we might still be able to save the Underdog."

Leesa's face crinkled with uncertainty. "You want to break the law in broad daylight, with thousands of people watching?"

They'd be a whole lot more likely to get caught, but as far as Marcus was concerned, a crime was a crime, no matter what time of day it was. And, more important, they had no other option.

"Yes."

"Let's do it!" Leesa was so excited she embraced him in an impulsive hug.

After adjusting his sling, Marcus hugged her back with his good arm. He could feel her hair tickling the skin at the collar of his hoodie, and when he shifted the mask the tiniest bit to let some air in, he caught a whiff of her peach shampoo. That meant that she could definitely smell the sweaty, sunscreeny, skateboard-greasy stink Marcus had going on. He pulled back, suddenly embarrassed.

He was glad he did—Antonio was looking at him like he was about to skin him alive.

"Leesa," the bigger kid said through gritted teeth. "What. Is. Going. On?"

Leesa gave him an abbreviated version of the plan— most of it was scrapped now that they weren't going to the cell block, anyway. And they were already running out of time.

"I'll explain more later," she said hurriedly. "Right

now, I just need you to borrow a truck and meet us at the—what's it called, Marcus?"

"The Hurt Door. It's the big red one."

The look Antonio shot him seethed with annoyance, but he didn't address Marcus.

"Leesa, that's insane. First off, who's going to give me their truck? I'm thirteen."

"Someone who owes your brother a favor. You're always bragging that his goons let you drive stolen cars. Tell them you're learning the family business."

Antonio's jaw tightened, but Marcus could tell he was starting to feel the pressure.

"Vince isn't going to like it," he muttered.

"So don't tell him!" Leesa said impatiently. "Antonio, you're my best friend." When she said that, something twitched at the side of the older kid's mouth. Marcus had the strange feeling that he was about to cry. If Leesa noticed, she didn't say anything. "Please . . ."

"Fine," Antonio said in a clipped tone. "I'll do my best."

"You're amazing!" Leesa cheered, and started to hug him, too, but Antonio shouldered past her. His lips were pursed and his face was sullen and he didn't make eye contact with either of them when he stalked off down the bridge.

Leesa looked a little upset but she didn't let that get in the way of her purpose. "Come on," she said to Marcus, her eyes shining with hope. "Let's go do something!"

Then she started to run, and Marcus ripped off his mask, sucked in air, and sprinted after her toward the Unnaturals Dome.

45

CASTOR WASN'T READY WHEN THE FIGHT DOOR OPENED.
He thought he'd have more time. More time to prepare.
More time to live.

He couldn't hope for the bell to rescue him from an
early end as it had rescued Enza, so Castor steeled himself to fight bravely and honor the other Unnaturals who
he hadn't been able to help escape. As he entered the
arena, the eagle-dog spead his wings wide and carried
his head high.

Then, the door on the other side of the Dome swung open and Laringo padded quietly, menacingly forward.

Castor realized that for all the time he'd spent staring at Laringo's poster, with the exception of a couple glimpses, he'd never truly seen Laringo face-to-face.

Castor needed time to study Laringo's movements, so he took to the air from the start. His flying was stronger now, and he'd learned to do enough tricks to impress the crowd when he wasn't fighting. He soared up, feeling the anticipation in the Dome building as he climbed higher and into the rafters. When he was nearly brushing against the ceiling, he shot down in a nosedive, his ears whipping back as he gained speed.

When Laringo reared up on his hind legs to slash at Castor with his razor claws, Castor shot underneath him, bucking up against his stomach. The white tiger was thrown into the air and flipped onto his back, and when the crowd erupted in impressed shouts at the Invincible's expense, Castor hoped that Pookie had been right.

Those cheers were his ticket out of here.

Castor flapped his powerful wings again, doing a tour for his fans. But he was already coasting in order to catch his breath, and Castor could feel the strain in his muscles. In the wind, his fur felt damp with sweat, and his tongue wagged as he gulped the air. He fluttered down on the opposite side of the ring, but Laringo had already turned to home in on him, and Castor knew his strength training had not been enough.

Castor could dip and dive and fly and soar, but all of that took energy, and Laringo was called the Invincible precisely because he was indefatigable.

The white tiger snarled and took off toward him. Castor stayed on all fours, planning to spring, Pookie style, at the last second, but Laringo adjusted for it this time, and the stinger arced over the smooth white head a beat early, stabbing downward right as Castor was jumping up.

Castor lurched clumsily to the side, rolling out of the way just in time. Laringo's tail smashed into the ground instead. He roared and whirled around, and Castor was on the defensive, his talons raking the sand as he scrabbled backward, and Laringo lunged after him with relentless jabs.

Castor knew Laringo was bred to fight like a machine to the very end, even if it meant running himself into the ground. How could he stop him? If he didn't do something drastic, at some point, he was going to get stung.

To win in the crowd's eyes, Castor needed something grand. He needed to *give them a show!*

The next time Laringo's stinger darted over his head,

Castor jumped forward to meet it. He clasped the seg-mented tail in his talons, wrenched hard to the right to spin the mutant tiger off his feet.

Castor had become an expert flier, but he wasn't used to lifting more than himself. The weight was almost more than he could bear. Still, he flapped his gray feath-ers hard, and slowly, he and Laringo rose together. The crowd was cheering like crazy, and Castor fluttered in the center of the ring, basking in the applause.

"Do it," Laringo sneered when they were near the golden Dome. He was still hanging upside down.

"Do what?" Castor asked.

"Do it. Drop me. Kill me." Laringo's velvet voice was shaky with emotion for once, and the awful request rat-tled Castor.

"No." Castor didn't want to kill anyone. Even Lar-ingo. "It's over."

"It's far from over. It's never over. To live here, you must keep killing. If I can't kill you, they'll find another animal who will. The only way for you to live today is to kill me." Laringo's tone had changed to a purring threat. Castor recognized it from when he'd promised Enza she wouldn't win against him, and everyone knew how that had turned out. Castor faltered a little.

"This isn't your fault," Castor told his captive. "Before

the scientists, before the serum, you were different. You can stop."

"Drop me, mutt," was Laringo's only reply.

Castor turned toward the virtual announcer, waiting for her to call the match, but to his alarm, she wasn't there. There was no one to call the match.

Or end it.

With stubborn resolve, he gritted his teeth and hung in the air for a few more minutes. But the muscles in his wings were quivering, and Laringo's tail was starting to slip from his talons. Finally, he dropped down to the ground and released Laringo, swooping away from the white tiger before he could take a swipe at him. But he didn't have anywhere to go and his energy was waning, and a tiny whisper of a thought snuck up on Castor as he scrambled away: *He was probably going to die.*

46

Marcus and Leesa stood outside the Hurt Door, waiting for Antonio.

They had taken the beach path to get to the outside of the Dome, climbing over slippery rocks and through prickly brush. They'd walked all around the circular stadium, and they were both sunburned and coughing when Marcus finally spotted the big red door—unguarded, out of the way, and with only one lock.

They would open it to free the animals as soon as

Antonio arrived with the transport truck. But the minutes were ticking by—inside, they could hear the cheers suggesting the match was under way.

Where was he?

Unlike Marcus, Leesa didn't have a gas mask, and her throat felt scratchy. She knew it wasn't safe to stay out here for much longer. Leesa jabbed the letters on her screen, texting Antonio for what felt like the millionth time.

> Antonio, please answer. Are you coming? What about the plan? What about the animals?

What she didn't type, but thought, anyway: *What about me?*

Finally, her pocket vibrated with a response.

> Too late.

What was that supposed to mean? Leesa started to ask why, but before she finished typing, another text appeared from Antonio. Leesa stared at it and felt the blood rushing in her ears.

"What does it say?" Marcus pulled the mask down to ask. He must've seen the panic on her face.

Leesa turned the tablet to show him what Antonio had written.

> Can't get the truck. They're already using it for scouting. All new mutants coming tomorrow.

"All new mutants?" Marcus scrunched up his already-pink face. "But it's still the middle of the season. Unless . . ."

He thought of the last bit of the headline: *special surprise.*

"Another Mash-up. Another slaughter," Leesa guessed miserably. "Give me the keys," she said, holding her hand out. "It's now or never."

But they couldn't seem to get the red door open. With dozens of keys on Pete's key ring and nothing identifying one from the other, every key seemed to be the wrong key.

"Let me try." Marcus shifted the giant key ring to select another one. Without the use of his left arm, it was an awkward maneuver, but he thought he might have more luck than Leesa. Nope.

"Don't force it. That one's rusted!" Leesa said impatiently. "We have to be almost at the end of the ring."

Marcus jiggled the ring, trying to get the last key unstuck, and the metal pieces clinged and clanged together noisily, the cacophony echoing their frustration.

"Those are for the individual cages. You need a different key."

Marcus froze and turned around.

"Pete," he said. It was all over now that they'd been caught, and Marcus had never imagined it could be so hard to look at his big brother. "I'm sorry. For what I said to Bruce. For getting you fired. For stealing your keys . . ." It felt like there was a clenched fist sitting inside his chest, and Marcus was afraid he was going to break down in front of Leesa. "I just wanted to make things better."

Pete shook his head and squeezed Marcus's shoulder. "No, you did the right thing. I'm the one who should be sorry. Some role model I am, when my kid brother can't even count on me to do what's right. When I saw you'd taken the keys, I wished I'd had the guts to do it. Now I can. Joni gave me these. She quit, too."

Pete pulled out a red key for the red door and slid it into the single lock. Then they heard a click, and their eyes grew wide.

"Got it." Pete grinned. "Ready?"

The two kids nodded, even though neither of them was quite sure what to expect. Together they pushed open the door, slow and sneaky, so they wouldn't be seen.

Not that there was a chance anyone would have noticed them. Inside, the most beloved mutant was fighting the most hated one, and everyone in the stands was on their feet, screaming. It seemed even more deafening than usual. Out of habit, Leesa looked up for Joni Juniper, who usually kept the crowd in check during the key parts of the match, but she was truly gone.

They didn't call the eagle-dog toward the door immediately; they needed to wait for a time when it was certain he could make it out. Leesa tried to make sense of what was going on in the ring. The fight was between the Invincible and the Underdog, but she felt like she was watching another match entirely—one from over a year ago, featuring Pookie the Poisonous.

"By the way," Marcus's brother said from behind them, "when I went to the Underdog's cell earlier, I found this. Did you leave it here before, Marcus?"

He pulled a book out of his back pocket, and Leesa's eyes lit up. "That's mine!" she squealed, snatching the cherished possession out of his hands. There was a small piece of web caught on the cover, and when Leesa touched the intricate thread, the silvery strands stuck to her fingers.

Pookie. He was alive.

Leesa looked back to the match, and as she watched the eagle-dog, really watched him, she was unable to shake a strong sense of déjà vu. When the Invincible swiped his claw low—a blow that might've gutted another fighter—the Underdog bent all four knees at once and pushed up into an impressive jump, aided by the sudden snap of his wings. Every time the eagle-dog flipped in the air, every time he jumped to block a strike, even the way he moved reminded her of Pookie.

The longer Leesa watched, the more surreal it got, because she realized the eagle-dog didn't just have a vague similarity to Pookie's style; he was using the exact same choreography. The same moves in the same order that Pookie had used when he'd fought the Invincible himself. And just like Pookie had learned that day, the eagle-dog was slowly figuring out that you couldn't beat a foe like this one with a backflip or a well-timed jump.

Leesa saw a flash of blue and yellow in her peripheral vision, and she turned to see an angry parrot flapping toward them.

"Alert, alert!" the bird squawked. "Security breach!"

"Perryyyy," Pete groaned. He swiped his arms, grasping for it, but the bird kept dodging him.

"ALERT!" the bird bellowed, beating its wings in Pete's face.

"He's going to blow our cover," Marcus said anxiously as people started to turn toward them and stare.

"It's me he wants." Pete sighed. "I'll lead him to the holding room. Joni's waiting for me there anyway—she wanted to help however she could. You guys get this show on the road. We've got your back."

The bird followed Pete, just like he said it would, and Marcus and Leesa looked at each other and took a deep breath.

"HEY!" they yelled, beckoning. "Over here! Underdog! The door is open!"

But they hadn't thought of the fact that the stadium would be way too loud for the competitors to hear them. Or that they'd be way too engrossed in a life-or-death match to be paying much attention to the crowd.

The Invincible might not be able to fly, but he had more strength, more energy, and more stamina than any other creature. The eagle-dog had tried to tire out the scorpion-tiger with his air attacks, but now that he was forced back to the ground, he had an immediate disadvantage.

The Underdog was panting, and his wing muscles were fatigued.

Meanwhile, the Invincible was just getting started.

Despite his exhaustion, the eagle-dog started to run. But a dog's stride was no match for a tiger's long, loping steps. And though the Underdog was good at weaving and dodging, his quick-footed turns were useless against the Invincible's unpredictable scorpion scuttle over the smooth terrain.

They zigzagged back and forth across the arena, and whenever the Underdog got close to being pinned against the wall, he'd have to take sudden flight. It didn't take long until each flap of his exhausted wings looked strenuous, and his body bobbed heavily in the air.

Finally, he lost control of flight completely, and the Underdog collapsed face-first on the floor of the arena. Still he did not want to give up, and he pulled his body forward with his front paws, his muscles sticky with sand. His wings dragged after him, limp and useless.

The Invincible stalked behind the Underdog, just a big cat ready to pounce now, and Leesa covered her mouth with one hand, trying not to scream, and Marcus clutched her other hand tightly.

After everything they'd done, was it really going to end like this?

The shadow of the Invincible's stinger hung over the Underdog now, but there was another shadow in the sand, and it got larger and more distinct as the form neared the ground on a gossamer thread. A bulbous shape, eight long legs.

"It's him!" Leesa shouted, clutching her book to her chest. If anyone could help the eagle-dog defeat the Invincible, it was the one creature who'd ever stood a chance against him: Pookie.

47

LARINGO WHIRLED AWAY FROM CASTOR WHEN HE HEARD the noise behind him, and when he saw Pookie in fighting stance, with his four front legs raised in the air and his prominent fangs exposed, every hair on the tiger's body seemed to ruffle up, and Castor could smell the stink of fear on him—the Invincible was afraid.

Afraid of Pookie.

"You can't win if Master's decided you should lose," Laringo insisted. The big cat bent over Castor, so close that Castor could see each of his whiskers, and smell the food on his breath—fresh meat.

"Maybe Eva Eris isn't a good master," Pookie called, diverting Laringo's attention. "Maybe it's time we let someone else decide. Maybe you should decide for yourself. Where is that tiger cub you once were, Laringo? Where is the beast he wanted to be?"

"Dead, like everyone else." Laringo narrowed his eyes. "Like you. Like your flying friend here. All dead."

He swung his tail to strike, but Pookie wouldn't give him the chance. He used his agile spider legs to spring into the air and landed softly, just outside the big cat's reach. But then Laringo shot after him, a blur of white speed, and it was only Pookie's erratic maneuvering on those eight legs that saved him.

Laringo's tail was stabbing down all around Pookie now, coming dangerously close to hitting him. Instead of running from it, Pookie jumped right at the scorpion tail, dancing up the segments while avoiding the deadly stinger.

His mentor wasn't using any of the techniques he'd shown him, Castor realized with alarm. Pookie's actions were not focused, or choreographed, or designed for the audience in any way. They were desperate, seeking out any weakness in this indestructible foe.

Laringo couldn't do much with Pookie attached to him, so he whipped his tail around like a lasso, trying to shake off the mutant spider. But Pookie's feet were sticky enough to hang from the ceiling, so they clung tightly to the thick tail.

Still, he couldn't hang on forever. Castor couldn't just lie here. He had to help him.

"I'm coming, Pookie," he promised, struggling to drag his wounded body up.

Before he got the chance, suddenly, Castor's whole body was on fire.

For a moment, Castor thought he'd been stung before realizing the pain was the power surging through the electric collar at his throat and into his body. Castor's muscles spasmed uncontrollably and his mouth foamed.

Pookie's collar had lit up with power, too, and his shaking body made Laringo's tail clatter.

"Looks like Master's decided," Laringo purred, and threw his body backward.

Laringo's back hit the ground with a thud, and Castor was sure Pookie was crushed beneath him.

Clearly, so was Laringo, so the scorpion-tiger was wholly unprepared when Pookie came sailing through the air on a thread from above to land on Laringo's chest, burying those red fangs deep inside Laringo's left shoulder. The cat let out a yowl like nothing Castor had ever heard before, and then his eyes rolled back.

"I told you Pookie would keep you safe," his tiny teacher said, and scuttled over to where Castor was lying. Castor was still panting from the ordeal, but he wagged his tail in ferocious gratitude. He reached the tip of his wing forward to rest it on Pookie's shoulder.

"How did you . . . ?" Castor started to ask, and Pookie grinned.

Instead of answering, he nodded toward the dark object lying discarded in the sand. It was the shock collar—he'd slipped his skinny neck right through.

"Oldest trick in the book!" The Chihuahua chuckled. "He'll be all right, by the way," Pookie said, glancing over at the big cat lying immobile in the sand. "I thought about what you said. That you are Castor and not a monster. Pookie isn't a monster, either. I didn't give him enough poison to kill—"

In the next moment, Laringo's eyes snapped open, and his last surge of strength sent his tail snapping like a thick whip, and the full force of it smashed into Pookie before Laringo shuddered to the ground unconcious. The crowd gasped, and before Castor could even tell what was happening, he heard a girl's heartbroken wail slice through the silence of the stadium: "Pookie!"

"No," Castor whined. "No . . ."

Pookie hadn't been stung, but he was small enough that the blow had crushed him. He lay still, but as Castor curled up in the sand next to his mentor and laid his head against Pookie's chest, he could still hear a faint, strained heartbeat.

"Don't go," he pleaded. "Just stay with me a little longer."

Pookie's eyelids fluttered open. When he saw Castor leaning over him, his mouth split into his familiar pointy-toothed grin, but it was only enough to reassure Castor for a moment. The smile turned into a grimace as the old dog started to cough—a wet, rattling rasp that sounded very grave indeed.

"You were right, young pup," Pookie wheezed. "We should've left when you said. The student has more wisdom than the teacher. Pookie's just an old cowardly fool, isn't he?"

"No!" Castor nosed the white, whiskery sides of his mentor's face with tender respect. "Never. You're the bravest dog I've ever known."

Pookie, the sky-born mini who loved humans and performing tricks, had saved his life.

"You're the brave one, Castor. That's what I came to tell you. Look."

His glassy eyes drifted up to rafters, and Castor saw a huge web glittering near the top of the domed roof. In beautiful, elaborate letters, he had woven CASTOR THE BRAVE.

"You wove words, like in the book." Castor smiled.

"I wanted you to see it at the end of the match, when you'd won. . . ." Pookie's breathing was getting shallower now, but his round eyes were fierce, and he spoke with urgency. "But winning is not what makes you brave, pup. Understand? It was in you from the start, and it is in you still. And you must use it to lead your pack out of here."

"You're my pack, Pookie. Come with us."

Pookie coughed harder and flecks of red speckled the front of his chest. When he spoke again, his voice was so faint Castor had to bend low to hear his words. "I'm afraid I'm going on a different journey, pup," he said weakly. "One I must make on my own."

Castor heard a whistle and turned his head. It wasn't the shrill sound the metal instruments made, though—it was a musical two-note signal, a sound just for Pookie.

"She's here," his mentor said. His eyes, always so quick and bright, were starting to cloud over, so he closed them. A little smile played across his pointy snout as he sighed, "Leesa came for me."

48

The world had seemed hazy and still while Castor held Pookie, but suddenly, everything clicked into sharp focus.

The lights, the people, the arena.

The girl running across the open field.

The boy, Marcus, running after her.

The crowd chanting, "Mash-up! Mash-up!" when the five doors slid open and the rest of Team Klaw and Team Scratch poured in.

But like Castor, with Laringo down for the count, they'd given up on the match. They didn't hear horns or see scores or wins or losses. They all saw the Hurt Door the human children had flung wide-open, and the whisper of green visible beyond it.

Go, Pookie had said. *GO!*

Castor forgot about his broken bones and foggy brain—he was on his feet in an instant.

"Come on!" His urgent bark roused the others—everyone but Rainner, who held back, and Deja, who had disappeared, and together they galloped toward the red door with its sliver of light.

Alarm bells were sounding as he ran, and that awful parrot was screeching for backup, but Castor could already smell the air outside, and everything pleasurable in his brain seemed to fire at once. Outside. The pollution and grease and sweat and meat and metal and dirt that blended in his memories of Lion's Head was right there in front of him, tickling his nose. And under that, he caught a whiff of musky freshness that made him think: *green.*

As Castor shouldered the door open for his new pack, he almost collapsed with the realization that he was really going to do it. He was going to reach the Green-plains, and soon.

Nothing could stop him now.

But then, the screams did. They were panicked screams, in-grave-danger screams, blood-frozen-inside-your-veins screams. And they were coming from Marcus—the blond boy who'd comforted him when he was hurt, the boy who had opened the door.

It took all the willpower Castor had to turn back toward that Dome, but when he pushed through the red door and saw the mutant tiger on his feet, with his deadly stinger stabbing toward Leesa, and Marcus sprinting after her, Castor's hackles rose, and protective instinct took over. As much as he wanted his freedom, he would not let Laringo kill Pookie's human, or the boy who was starting to feel like his friend. As far as he was concerned, they were both part of his pack.

Castor turned abruptly and started tearing across the field.

He was surprised to see the rest of his teammates turn as well. "You should go!" he insisted, but his friends would not leave him. They flanked him, forming a wide protective barrier, and ran as one to finally put a stop to the vicious Laringo.

49

LEESA WAS HUNCHED OVER HER PET'S TINY, BROKEN form, and she didn't appear to see the danger around her, no matter how loudly Marcus screamed. The Invincible seemed to have risen from the dead, and he was gathering strength to attack. Meanwhile, the Underdog was speeding toward Marcus, talons raised.

Perhaps they were both about to die?

Marcus ducked in terror, but instead of skewering him like Marcus feared, the eagle-dog hooked his talons in Marcus's collar and lifted him off the ground. Then the Underdog shot back across the Dome, dove down sharply, and snatched up Leesa just as the scorpion-tiger swiped.

"AHHHH!" they both screamed as the dog veered upward again.

Marcus's stomach lurched as the ground receded, his legs kicked at the air for purchase, his hair whipped around his face, and his heart was racing so fast he thought it might explode and kill him. That is, if he didn't fall to his death first.

But after a couple of seconds of dangling in the eagle-dog's sure grip, Marcus stopped worrying so much about dying and started freaking out about the fact that he was *flying*. Yeah, it was the most terrifying thing he'd ever experienced, but it was also thrilling and amazing. He could see everything from up here—the entire bowl of the stadium, the stands full of people going nuts, a holographic picture of the Unnaturals banner and the light post just beyond it, where Leesa and Antonio watched the games. And he could see the mutants fighting on the field.

They were all charging against the Invincible.

The Enforcer gripped the base of the scorpion tail in a powerful, tentacled fist. The Invincible might've found the strength to sting, if the bull wasn't butting his head with crushing force. In front of him, the rabbit-panther was feinting left and right with amazing speed, keeping the champion distracted.

Then, suddenly, all of the mutant animals—including the one that held them in his clutches a hundred feet in the air—started convulsing. Their collars were shocking them! The Underdog lurched left and then right, and Marcus saw the lights blur and the walls whirl. Marcus thought they might smash into the ground, but then the eagle-dog's flying leveled.

Glancing down, Marcus could see Pete waving and holding something—the Swift's collar! He'd cut the shock electricity to the collars. Joni was down there with him, and she was quickly pulling off the other mutants' collars.

Marcus reached up behind him, his fingers searching the fur around the eagle-dog's head. He found the collar and unbuckled it, and the Underdog immediately barked his gratitude. Then he bent forward and licked the side of Marcus's face in a slobbery, wet kiss.

"Finally free," he heard Leesa's voice say over the wind. He looked to where she was dangling beside him, and saw her holding a small collar in her fist as well. Tears leaked down her face, but Marcus was relieved to see that his friend was smiling. "I hope wherever Pookie is, he's feeling this free."

50

Now that he'd saved the kids, Castor knew it was time to join his friends.

He didn't want to leave the children in the stands because without the matchmaker to maintain order, it was absolute chaos, with panicked people pushing and shoving, desperate to get away from the freed mutants. He knew Marcus and Leesa would be safe with Pete, though, so when he spotted the medic waving from the side of the arena far away from the showdown with

Laringo, Castor swooped down low and unclenched his talons, dropping them lightly at his feet. Then he circled back around the Dome, zooming toward his pack.

"What's going on?" Castor asked. Laringo had escaped the group attack when the shocks went off. Now, he was prowling in front of Castor's friends, and the animals seemed oddly hypnotized.

"I can't stop." Laringo's voice was soft as he addressed the survivors—almost a purr. "I told you, just like I told Pookie. But you wouldn't listen." He started to circle, and Castor could sense Jazlyn trembling beside him.

He didn't blame her. For a mutant who was so strictly trained, the Invincible felt like the electric collar at your throat—you were never sure when it was going to go off or how devastating it would be. Castor realized that Laringo's collar didn't work any more than his did now.

"You're as free as any of us," Castor tried to reason one last time, keeping his eyes locked on Laringo's. He gestured his head toward the door. "So you *can* stop if you want to."

Castor heard the angry rush of air from Moss's nostrils. It was clear the bull didn't like the idea of Laringo leaving with them very much at all.

Neither did Laringo.

"Us?" The big white cat started to stalk back and

forth in front of them, his scorpion's stinger hanging idly at the air. "There is no us. There is only Master."

Couldn't he understand that there didn't have to be a master, either?

"You've killed enough," Moss said, grinding his square teeth as he listed their names. "Firan . . . Buzzle . . . Pookie . . ." Beside Castor, the bull began to weep.

His eyes dilated, the pale blue turned to black, and Laringo's translucent tail started to curl forward over his back. "No," Laringo insisted. He cocked his head, as if listening to someone whispering. "Master's displeased," he said, and any emotional connection the tiger had once had seemed to have completely vanished from his soul. "I've still got to kill all of you."

As outnumbered as Laringo was, his detached words could still strike terror in the other animals' hearts, and Castor's teammates tensed, nervous about who that scorpion's tail might lunge at next.

Enza didn't give him half a chance. The injured grizzly lived up to her namesake and told Laringo in a truly fearless growl, "You're not going to get the chance to kill anyone, you sorry excuse for a feline. Not ever again."

But instead of lunging at her nemesis, Enza turned sharply to the right and slammed her broken, bruised, but still powerful body into the light post. All of the pole battering she'd done during training in the Pit must've paid off, because the hit was so hard the clang of cracking metal shuddered around the stadium.

"Do it," Laringo challenged.

Now it was Samken's turn. The Enforcer thundered forward and smashed his broad, hard head into the pole.

This time, the post swayed dangerously, but then it came to a stop.

"I'm protected, you see? Invincible."

The words sounded desperate and Castor was bewildered, remembering how Laringo had begged him to end his life.

"No one's invincible," Moss said. "Not even you." The zebra-bull gave the post a swift hind kick, and finally, the blow was just enough to wrench the light pole from its foundation.

"No!" a woman's voice thundered through the loudspeaker as the light post began to tip. "My champion!"

Castor and his friends were scrambling out of the way, but Laringo wasn't even looking at the falling pole. The scorpion-tiger stared up at the box seats, and Castor recognized the woman he'd seen at every match—the woman with hair the color of blood, standing out like a lion's mane around her head.

It was her voice that was calling to Laringo. And now

it was Laringo who was hypnotized.

"Master," the scorpion-tiger purred serenely, and then Castor shut his eyes against the awful crunch of metal as the light pole fell.

Castor felt vibrations from the impact traveling up through his feet, but when he opened his eyes, he saw it had just missed him.

Laringo hadn't been so lucky. The post lay right where he'd been standing, and all that was left of the big cat was the tip of his spiked tail, peeking out from underneath the metal. Castor swore he saw a twitch, but he wasn't going to stick around to find out.

Fans were screaming and stampeding toward the exit, and Horace was now at the Hurt Door with two dark-haired, scowling teen boys. For a second, Castor was too overwhelmed to move.

Had he lost his chance?

But then he noticed the massive crater of a hole in the floor where the post had snapped off its foundation.

An exit.

He locked eyes with Enza. "The next time you see an open door . . . ," he said, and his friend nodded warily.

"In there," Castor instructed his teammates. "Quick!"

The darkness made Samken nervous. "But we have no idea what's down there," he protested, his front tiptoes teetering on the edge as he peered down into the darkness. "It could lead anywhere."

"I guess we'll find out together, Sammy," Jazlyn said. "No time like the present." She bounded forward and pushed the big gray rump, and together they tumbled into the abyss.

"Get them!" the red-haired woman snarled over the speakers.

"Get, get, get!" Perry echoed, circling around again and buzzing near their heads like an annoying fly. "Alert, alert, alert!"

Castor saw Whistlers like Slim and blue-coated Bruce making their way through the tide of people. On the other side, he knew Horace and his two muscled boys would reach them soon. It was time to go.

"Your turn," Castor told Enza, but the grizzly's clunky cast got stuck on the way down. "Hurry," Castor barked.

Finally, she managed to squeeze through, and Castor turned to wave Moss after her. But the veteran wasn't behind him. He saw him across the stadium, letting the kids climb onto his back.

"What are you doing?" Castor yipped as the bull galloped by. "You have to come with us!"

But Moss was adamant. "For so long I did nothing." He said with a shake of his horns. "Now I need to do this.

I need to protect them. For Pookie."

Castor couldn't argue with honor. He reached up his snout to lick the children's hands, but there wasn't much time for good-byes—in the next instant, an army of handlers and blue-coated Whistlers arrived.

"GO!" Moss told Castor as he reared up on his hind legs to protect the kids on his back. Then he looked at the enemies around him, lowered his head, and before a single person could reach for a gold whistle, he charged.

Now that's brave, Castor thought. As the panicked Whistlers scattered and the stands emptied out, he nodded a thanks to his valiant friend. Then Castor, the Unnatural bird-dog, turned, barked, and jumped toward his freedom.

EPILOGUE

Your paws pound the cracked pavement. With each breath, you pull short sips of recycled air into your lungs. Your shoulder muscles keep rhythm as your legs shoot out in front of you. Again. Again. Faster. Don't stop.

Around you, others echo your progress. Paws, claws, hooves.

No footsteps, though: no men. Not yet.

There is no alpha in this pack. You each take a turn to follow and to lead. You draft behind your friend when you are tired. You stop to help one another up when you fall. And when all seems lost, you work together to find the path again. In this pack, all are equal, all are family. All are free.

Together, you run through an unfamiliar new city. Up above, you know the mirrored blocks the men made are rising high into the clouds, but down here, ceiling replaces sky, and light panels replace sun. Otherwise, this underground city is not much different from where you began. You still recognize the sound of a bone machine, and the smell of a rotten river, but you are not afraid. You can read people's signs and pack lines alike. You know how to find food and where to find shelter in alleyways. You know how to stay alive.

And, with your collar off, you are more alive than you've ever been. You don't know what risks lie ahead or what troubles you may face. You don't know the secrets of the green forest, but you don't care. For now, what you know is freedom.

Your tail wags behind you. Your tongue flops against your smiling jaws, trailing spit in the wind. You inhale the rank stench of garbage in the street, and delight in the scratchy film of pollution at the back of your throat. You love all of it, because it cannot be contained or put in a cage.

You pause to lift up your voice in song, to call to your brothers, wherever they are, and tell them your story. Once, you thought you'd come home to them, but now you know you can never go back. You know something else is out there, a place without the hard street lines or the men's hard rules, a place with a lot more green.

Together, you and your team push forward, a blur of feathers and horns, hopes and fears. You keep searching for the route that will lead you to the other side of the river, to the wild forest that you remember from dreams, sprawling and untamed.

Only this time, it won't be a dream. Around the next corner, or the next, you know you'll see it, plain as the fur on your faces.

It's there.

It's real.

It's waiting for you.

ACKNOWLEDGMENTS

FOR STARTERS, THANK YOU, EVERYONE AT KATHERINE Tegen Books, for all of your hard work carrying this project from pitch to finished book. I especially want to thank my talented editors, Claudia Gabel, from whose brain Castor flew, winged and wonderful, and Melissa Miller, who made him soar. I owe you both so much for your sustained faith, which amazes me still. Your grace and good humor saved this book, and likely my writing career with it. And Alex Arnold, who I'm sure worked some Pookie-esque behind-the-scenes magic, know that I appreciate it! I couldn't ask for a better publishing team.

To "Ms. Soup," without whom I never would've started writing in the first place, and Andrea Spooner, without whom I never would've come back to it, I owe a whole lot.

To James Patterson, a living legend: thanks for giving a newbie like me a shot. You taught me so much about storytelling and work ethic, and I'll be forever grateful. Still working on cutting out some of those poetic flourishes, but hey, it's a process!

Siobhan, Kate, and Connie, thank you for your endless encouragement and advocacy. You're the women I aspire to be.

Thanks to my parents and sisters for the steady stream of love, particularly in the form of messages on "group channel" that make me laugh until my stomach aches.

Many thanks to my bluetick pup, the Hellhound, Bertie. With bounding excitement, aggressive affection, a cocked head or a whipping tail, raised hackles or yogic stretches, and various yips, barks, snarls, and howls, you helped me bring Castor and his pack to life. You've also been a champion snuggler during all those hours I've spent at the computer, trying to get this story just right. How about I forgive the shredded window screens and gutted couch, and we'll call it even?

And finally, most of all, to my husband, Adlai: thank you for putting up with this writing life. For making me another coffee and cooking me another meal during all those late nights and early mornings. For taking the dog out or going to the event alone when I was on a roll and needed to write just one more paragraph. For the bottles of cheap bubbly to mark each milestone, no matter how small. For every expression of support and declaration of love. Without you, I'd never make it to the last page.

THE BATTLE CONTINUES IN

Read on for a sneak peek of the epic finale.

THE CREATURE OPENED HER EYES AND WAS NEARLY BLINDED by the bright light. *Still daytime.*

She hugged her gray wings tighter around her body and shrank back into their darkness, trying to hold on to the dream—if you could call it that. She was never sure if it was dream or memory or just a story she told herself. Whether she'd really even been asleep.

"I've gotta split," one of the humans announced. The creature recognized the voice. It was Vince, the trainer.

The creature poked her head out. More than a hundred feet below her, the other mutant animals were back inside their cages, and the humans were packing up the lab, disinfecting the harnesses, swabs, and tools. Today's trials were already over.

The creature breathed a sigh of relief. So she had slept for most of the day, after all.

"Keep an eye on my Kill Clan," Vince called over his shoulder to one of the six researchers. They all dressed in crinkly yellow from head to toe and wore paper masks over their faces, so the creature couldn't tell them apart.

"Lazy Draino," whispered one of the Yellow Six, an older man. Thanks to her large, triangular ears, the creature had excellent hearing.

"He's just going to the bookies to gamble on tomorrow's big Unnaturals match," another human in yellow, this one a woman, answered.

The creature noticed that although the researchers always grumbled about Vince after he'd gone, they didn't say these things when he was around. She also noticed that Vince was the only one who could control the animals after they became mutants. Each group seemed to be getting more violent than the last.

"Are you going to watch it?" the man asked, coiling

up the breathing tube they used to test lung capacity. "The Underdog versus the Invincible?"

"No, but my kids will warp into the match, I'm sure. They're major Moniacs. My daughter really likes that eagle-dog."

"Doesn't have much of a chance, does he? Remember what happened last season? If they're just going to let the scorpion-tiger destroy all the other mutants, what's the point?" Only his eyes were visible above the mask, and the glasses he wore reflected the light like mirrors. To the creature, the man looked like a fat yellow fly.

"Hey, those ticket sales pay for our research." The woman held up a glass tube and shook it. "And it's not like we haven't seen worse in here."

They glanced toward the far end of the space, where a chain-link fence ran the length of the room. No longer useful, the mutants that had already failed the genetic tests mingled freely on the other side. The fence clinked and bulged as bodies pressed against it. They always got restless after Vince left.

"We should get going," the woman in yellow said nervously. They were the last two of the Yellow Six left. The man collected his jar of samples and hurried out after her, clicking off the lights on his way out the door.

3

Their day of work had ended, but the creature's was just beginning. She had a long night of hunting ahead of her.

She shook the stiffness out of her wings and the sleep out of her eyes, and then she clenched her toes on the metal slats of the vent to swing herself back upright. From her high perch, she surveyed the room below, wondering where to start. Since she rarely let herself be seen during the day, the creature had to gather everything that would sustain her under the cloak of darkness.

The other animals were still settling down, so first she crept to the corners of the room to check the traps she had set for wayward mice. Finding nothing there, she trotted over between the rows of stacked cages, her four legs making long, swift strides as she stalked her prey. Spotting the dart of a shadow, the creature pounced!

Her paws landed squarely on the fattest, juiciest cockroach she had ever seen. Dinner was served. She let out a little screech of happiness, but the way it echoed back to her ears sounded strangely flat, and instead of chowing down on the roach, she paused, looking at the empty cage in front of her.

That was where the panda had been—the one the Yellow Six called Mai. They must've finally taken her for the injection today.

4

The creature didn't usually get to know the new animals. They rarely stayed in the individual cages long before they were turned into mutants and moved to the other side of the fence in the group pen, dazed and bloodthirsty. And besides, she was different from them—she was nighttime, while they were daytime; she soared in the rafters, while they cowered in cages—and she preferred to keep her distance.

But the panda had lasted through eight versions of the serum without being pulled for testing. The Six seemed to like her. They were always cooing over her big, fluffy head and her perfect round ears and her curious, coal-rimmed eyes.

The creature just thought Mai's eyes looked sad. And sometimes at night, the creature would hear Mai singing songs to herself in the darkness, and those sounded sad, too. The creature avoided the area near the cages when the caged bear sang, letting the cockroaches skitter by unchecked.

Now, the creature looked down at her front paws and realized the juicy king cockroach had gotten away, too. In her surprise about Mai, she must've relaxed her grip.

Maybe the serum was successful this time, she thought hopefully, as she unfolded her wings and took to the air. *Maybe it did whatever Bruce and the Yellow Six hoped it would do, instead of turning sweet Mai into a snarling, red-eyed monster.* But as the creature swooped down to feast on the flies that buzzed above the warm, sleeping bodies, she heard a commotion on the other side of the lab.

There was growling and frenzied movement behind the fence, and the creature heard Mai's voice, no longer musical. It was changed by madness, or changed by pain. The creature knew that the herd in the group pen often turned on new additions and hoped that wouldn't happen to Mai.

Sometimes, when Vince arrived in the early mornings to train his "Clan," the creature saw him removing injured animals from the pen after he changed the water.

The creature didn't want to see him dragging out Mai's body. She didn't want to see the Yellow Six coaxing other frightened animals from their cages and snapping them into the harnesses to run their trials. She didn't want to see Bruce, and hear the *click click* of his pen after each injection, when he'd write down what happened.

This time, she especially didn't want to see What Happened.

She had a while yet before she'd hear the buzz of the overhead lights on their timers announcing the humans' coming arrival. She could still get some good hunting in.

But the creature had lost her appetite, and she already felt exhausted.

She flapped her wings and watched the space between herself and the other mutants grow, until what she had thought was a bear footprint now looked like nothing more than a shadow on the floor. The creature retreated back into her high perch, out of sight.

The creature hooked her feet into the vent in the ceiling to hang upside down. The rush of blood to her head was instantly calming, and she sighed. She clutched her tawny orange tail to her chest for its soft comfort, and wrapped her wings around herself, shutting out the world. Flexing her toes to make her body sway, the creature was beginning to rock herself back into a familiar dream.

And that's when the room exploded.

2

Perhaps the room had not actually exploded. But that was certainly how it felt. There was a terrible sound, and then the creature felt the crack vibrate up the walls and through her body.

She poked her head out of the tent of her wings to see what was going on below. She thought it must be the humans, trying out some new test, but the walkway outside the door was still silent, the lab still dark. Below her, the docile animals were milling around their cages with dazed expressions. Across the room, she could see the agitation of the more violent mutants as bits of plaster rained down around them. The explosion had come from behind the fence.

The creature followed the dust storm and discovered a fresh hole in the wall—a wall that, until this moment, had seemed as constant and indestructible as the humans. Out of the hole slithered a snake, its scales covered in the white powder.

The snake coiled herself up, her diamond-shaped head lifting to take in her surroundings. When she saw the other mutants, the snake froze.

The other animals froze, too, but an almost imperceptible shiver went through them, and even without seeing them, the creature knew that their pupils were dilating.

The creature thought of the reaction as the "kill drive," and she had seen it activated many times. It usually happened during research trials with the Yellow Six, or else in one-on-one fights Vince set up in the smaller pen when he needed to make room for new mutants. They were probably still hyped up from attacking Mai.

The creature couldn't remember how she'd escaped from Bruce and the Yellow Six, but she knew she didn't have the kill drive, or the indifference to pain that went with it. That's why she lived most of her life alone, high up in these rafters, keeping far away from everyone.

She would not want to be in the snake's position right now.

Sensing the danger she was in, the snake shot away from the other animals. She was quick and skilled at slithering between their feet, but there were many, many mutants, and soon she was backed into a corner against the fence, her tongue flicking and her tail rattling as they advanced on her with herky-jerky movements.

At least it would be over quickly.

But just as her attackers started to hurl themselves at her, two hidden slits opened on the snake's back, and a pair of wings snapped out between the scales. In the next instant, the snake took flight.

Other than herself, the creature had never seen another mutant fly. Many of them had wings, but they were too dazed, or too restricted, or too sick to use them. The creature's wings were made of thin, gray skin stretched out over tiny bones. They were flexible and scalloped on the bottom, allowing her to maneuver easily through the air. The snake's wings were different— rounded and delicate, with swirling patterns—like some of the insects the creature caught at night.

And like those moths she hunted, the flying snake

seemed to be attracted to the overhead lights, even though they were dimmed. The snake floated up and up, and the creature was too mesmerized to realize it was headed right for her!

"Hey! How do I get out?" the snake demanded, suddenly face-to-face.

"What?" gasped the creature, still upside down, peering out fearfully over her wrapped wings.

Despite being in a room with hundreds of other mutants, no one ever talked to her—she wasn't sure most of them *could* talk—and she spent most of her waking hours in darkness, alone. Now, this new animal was not only speaking to her, but it was asking her something that didn't make any sense. And it was not asking very nicely.

"Out!" the snake repeated. "I know you can't be deaf with those big ears. Where's-s-s the way outside?"

The creature had no idea what this strange snake was hissing about, but it was pressing closer and closer to her, and the creature felt too frightened to take flight.

"I don't want to hurt you. But I will." The snake's eyes were a light milky gray, like hard glass. "All I want is to get home."

Home?

It was a human word. That was where the Yellow

Six talked about going at night. She couldn't understand why anyone would want go where they were. But the snake was baring her fangs and rattling her tail now, and the creature knew if she didn't answer soon, something very bad was going to happen—if not with the snake, then with the humans. The lights would be clicking on any minute now, and when Vince arrived and saw the snake, the creature would be discovered, too.

"The humans go through those two doors," the creature answered finally, gathering her courage. "There." She pointed one of her white-tipped paws down toward the EXIT sign. "And there." She gestured across the room, to the door marked *H*.

The snake's diamond-shaped head was already zigzagging in dissent. "I don't care where the humans go. Everyone knows humans don't go into the s-s-sun," she hissed. "I mean the way *outside*. A tunnel through the walls. To the desert. Or the Greenplains-s-s."

Greenwhat? The creature's world was white walls and steel cages. The brightest color she'd encountered was the yellow of the scientists' suits.

"The only tunnel I've seen is the one you made. I, um, don't think that there *is* a way out."

"WHAT?" the snake shouted the word so loudly that her jaws unhinged. "There has-s-s to be. Moss's stories-s-s about escaped Unnaturals, Castor's babble about freedom . . . it can't all end here in another lab."

The overhead lights switched on, one by one, casting a pale, greenish glow over the room.

"They're coming," the creature warned. "You should go back to where you came from—wherever that is."

"Back to NuFormz?" the snake scoffed, glancing at the hole she'd slithered out of. "Back to prison, to fighting for human enjoyment, to a dumb eagle-dog talking nonsense about teamwork, when my team never cared a lick about me? Never."

Teamwork. The unfamiliar idea echoed in the creature's ears. "It must be better than here," she murmured.

Turning away, the snake careened around the ceiling, her moth wings fluttering erratically as she flung herself into the far corners of the room and veered too close to the fans. The creature was grateful that the snake would be preoccupied far away from her when the humans came.

Of course, now the snake was zooming back toward her. The creature saw the flick of forked tongue and the flash of fang and winced, preparing for the snake's venomous strike. Instead, the snake looked past her with narrowed eyes.

"That. There."

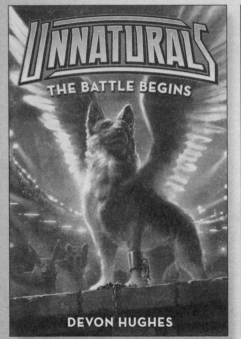